CHRISTMAS IN ATLANTIS WITH BONUS ANNOTATED COPY OF THE GIFT OF THE MAGI

A POSEIDON'S WARRIORS PARANORMAL ROMANCE

ALYSSA DAY

HOLLIDAY PUBLISHING

ATLANTIS

After eleven thousand years beneath the seas, the lost continent is lost no more. The fabled group known as Poseidon's Warriors will continue their sworn task of protecting humanity, but some things will change . . .
This year, Atlantis will celebrate its first-ever Christmas, and one of Poseidon's chosen will never, ever be the same.

1

———

ONE DOLLAR AND EIGHTY-SEVEN CENTS. That was all. And sixty cents of it was in pennies. Pennies saved one and two at a time by bulldozing the grocer and the vegetable man and the butcher until one's cheeks burned with the silent imputation of parsimony that such close dealing implied. Three times Della counted it. One dollar and eighty-seven cents. And the next day would be Christmas.

There was clearly nothing to do but flop down on the shabby little couch and howl. So Della did it. Which instigates the moral reflection that life is made up of sobs, sniffles, and smiles, with sniffles predominating.

-- The Gift of the Magi, O. Henry (1917)

*J*t was a bad damn day to be a pirate.

The storm had sprung full force from Poseidon's wrath or from the gates of the nine hells themselves. Seranth had only had time to give Dare a glimmer of a warning—an insistent pulse in the back of his mind before she even materialized on the deck.

Warning! Danger!

Seranth. The sea spirit who'd chosen him less than a year after he'd first captained a ship. Her thoughts and feelings were tied to him as closely as his own breath, and he'd risked her very existence in this stupid move. For *money.* Nothing more than stupid greed and avarice that might cost him the magical bond that had made him the best captain on the high seas.

And worse—sudden pain stabbed through his chest when he realized another, awful truth—he might never see Lyric again.

He shouted orders to his crew, even knowing that they couldn't hear him over the raging fury of the storm. He was drenched, water pouring from his head into his eyes, hindering his vision, but he kept at it. His crew was highly trained, and they all loved the *Luna* as much as he did. They were all working their asses off to save her.

He could feel Seranth reaching out to the heart of the storm; trying to calm the waves. She was a water elemental and could commune with the ocean at the best of times, but...

These were far from the best of times.

He'd listened to her immediately—taken action immediately—but immediately had been far too late.

Now rain lashed his crew, pummeled the deck, and threatened to drown them all with silvery sheets of pounding water. The waves threatened to swamp them. The ship was buffeted by the crests and valleys of mountainous waves. He kept shouting his futile orders to the crew, knowing they couldn't hear them, but driven to save the ship that was his entire life. He had to save them—must save them *all.*

His crew. The exotic supernatural creatures in his cargo. Seranth.

Saving himself fell into a distant fifth, or sixth, or hundredth place. Did he even deserve salvation? Probably not.

Hells, no.

He shouted out a bark of laughter that went unheard and lashed himself to the wheel. "Come and get me then, you bitch," he shouted at the ocean. "I've always known you'd claim me in the end."

The bow of his ship smashed into the crest of a monster wall of water, and he could feel the battering of her timbers and beams in his blood and bones. The *Luna*'s first mate was waving his arms to get Dare's attention. The man pointed to the boxes and bales of cargo lashed to the deck and to the temporary pen they'd built for their most precious cargo, who'd refused to go below where at least they would have been marginally safer.

Siberian unicorns are claustrophobic, the seller had said.

The creatures themselves had proven that 'claustrophobic' was a severe understatement. They'd made it very clear in no uncertain terms that they would not be put down in the hold of the ship. One of his crew had a broken leg and black eye to prove it; another had been knocked unconscious by flailing silver hooves.

Smitty was right. They needed to protect the animals. They were possibly the most valuable cargo Dare had ever carried on his ship. Beyond that, he had no wish to see such rare and beautiful creatures harmed. He was a pirate, not a monster.

He gave Smitty the thumbs-up, and his crew jumped into action, untying the cargo and hurling boxes into the sea. They'd been overloaded and were riding too low in the water as it was. They needed more maneuverability to get out of this. Profit be damned.

The wheel fought him like a wild thing; tried to yank itself out of his hands and turn the ship in pursuit of what he didn't know. Maybe the ship had decided to steer itself straight to the nine hells. Or send him and all his crew to visit Davy Jones. Or at least to visit the ghosts of past Atlantean sea captains.

Another monster wave was coming right for them. There was no way to maneuver around or through it. It was going to smash them into splinters. He threw his entire weight into steering the ship, turning it just a little to approach the wave at an angle.

It was the only chance they had.

A high-pitched screaming sent sound waves like rusty nails through his teeth and skull. He whipped his head to the side and saw catastrophe in the making. One of the sides of the unicorns' pen had come down, and the animals had pushed through, kicking and flailing in their terror. Ropes from the cargo's wooden boxes had tangled around the animals' feet, and the larger one—the male—was being pulled inexorably to the edge of the deck. His mate was screaming that horrible, visceral sound and trying to block her mate's slide across the deck.

Dare yanked his dagger out of its sheath and sliced through the rope holding him to the wheel. He *had* to save them—they didn't deserve to die for his folly.

He ran across the deck, pushing forward with a combination of bullheaded stubbornness and the practice of long years spent maneuvering his way around the ship. He launched himself through the air for the last few feet and landed flat on the deck, his reaching hands just grasping the end of the rope. He yanked hard, rolled over, and pushed himself to his feet. Then he twisted the rope around his waist to help give him leverage to pull.

Seranth! Turn us into that wave at just the right angle, or we're done for.

For the first time since he'd known the elemental, the sound of her voice in his mind was tinged with an undercurrent of fear:

I'll do my best, but my best might not be good enough in this instance. If that's the case, please know that my time with you has been a bright spot in millennia of existence.

It's not over yet, he thought at her fiercely, while maintaining his hold on the tangled unicorn and pulling the creature back bit by bit from the edge of the deck.

"We're going to hit!" he shouted, not even sure who was shouting at. Maybe only himself—or maybe Poseidon, who was in charge of the sea and so was ultimately responsible. After all, the sea god should favor the sons of Atlantis, or at least keep an eye out for them. Knowing Poseidon, he was probably drunk in some Olympian Tavern.

Bastard.

The ship hit the wall of water at an angle and – for just a moment—Dare thought they might actually survive it.

Then the rope ripped through his hands, tearing the skin from his palms, and spun him around with the force of its movement. When he turned, he was just in time to see the backsides of the animals as they went over the side.

He didn't even think; he just ran. He leaped up onto the railing, balanced precariously for a second to get a fix on where they were, and then dove into the churning water.

There was no chance he could save them.

There was less chance he could save himself.

But he'd be *damned* if he wouldn't try. The current took them immediately and slammed him into the side of the boat. Lights whirled around in spots before his eyes: kalei-doscopes of color alternating with terrifying darkness. He was fighting so hard to catch his breath that he almost didn't notice the warmth of the blood pouring down the side of his head when he clawed his way out from under the water. He saw the animals, which was a miracle itself, and they were swimming away from him and the foundering ship.

Of course they were. Because they had a lot more sense than he did.

He headed in their direction and managed to catch the end of the female's trailing rope. The ship loomed large and black behind them, and he realized he might've jumped out of a sinking ship and right into the maelstrom that was sinking it.

He kicked harder until he reached the animals, who were both flailing in the churning water, frantic with fear.

"It's going to be okay," he lied. Nothing was going to be okay ever again, but he didn't know how to speak unicorn anyway.

Also, he'd quite possibly cracked his skull open, because his mind wasn't making any sense at all.

Their names. What were their *names*?

The storm had pounded everything out of his mind, but he forced himself to think, wrapping one arm around the female's neck...*right*. English aristocracy. Some book. Ringley? No...

"*Bingley*. Bingley and Jane. We're going to be okay, guys. Somehow, we're going to be okay."

The storm suddenly, miraculously, began to dissipate. Either Seranth had been successful, or the ocean's fury was simply worn out from throwing its full force at the ship.

The *Luna* was limping toward him. Beaten and battered —almost, but not quite, broken. In the startling way of storms at sea, the sky had gone from darkest night back to daylight in the space of minutes. The waves were calming, the wind slowing, and he had the impossible thought that they might actually survive this.

Jane took that moment to kick him squarely in the groin, and he doubled over, gasping and choking when his face hit the water. When his ears quit ringing, he could hear Smitty shouting something at him from the broken side of the deck where the unicorns had gone over.

Dare looked up, still hunched in the water, and Smitty shouted again.

"Okay there, Cap'n?"

"Outstanding," he managed to yell back. "You want to throw down the dinghy so we can get Bingley and Jane back on board?"

"Right away, sir," his mate yelled.

"Did you hear that, you rotten nut-kickers? We're going to be okay," he choked out.

The unicorns looked dubious, if that's how you translated eyes rolling in their sockets and frantic hooves flailing. He put a hand over his crotch just in case, but then he had a hard time staying afloat, so he gave up and hoped lightning —or unicorn hooves—didn't strike twice.

Smitty shouted something else. Dare looked up instead of around, so he only peripherally saw the piece of wood that slammed into the back of his head.

Darkness.

Cold.

Freezing, icy, dark.

Swirling, floating, sinking.

Drowning.

Drowning.

When Dare came to, he was deep, deep beneath the

surface. His survival instinct's first instinct was to breathe, which was a horrible mistake. He choked and tried to force water out of his mouth and nose but it was impossible.

He couldn't see any light, he didn't know which was up and which was down, and even with superior Atlantean lung capabilities, he was pretty damn sure he was going to be dead in about the next five seconds. Even if the ship had been able to wait around for him, he'd never be able to reach it.

There was only one thing left to do, and luckily he knew how to do it, underwater or not.

He focused his mind and called for the Atlantean portal, which had been the only means of transport to the surface during the eleven thousand years Atlantis had been sunk beneath the seas.

I need you now.

The faint glow that heralded the portal's arrival began to manifest in front of him, but it was another case of too little, too late. Even the magic of Atlantis couldn't save him now. He tried to hang on—lungs bursting, head pounding with pain—but his vision of the swirling portal was narrowing to a point of light in the far distance. The lack of air was crushing his lungs. His last thought before the dark claimed him was that he only had one regret about dying.

He'd wanted to see Lyric one more time.

W hile the mistress of the home is gradually subsiding from the first stage to the second, take a look at the home. A furnished flat at $8 per week. It did not exactly beggar description, but it certainly had that word on the lookout for the mendicancy squad.

In the vestibule below was a letter-box into which no letter would go, and an electric button from which no mortal finger could coax a ring. Also appertaining thereunto was a card bearing the name "Mr. James Dillingham Young."

The "Dillingham" had been flung to the breeze during a former period of prosperity when its possessor was being paid $30 per week. Now, when the income was shrunk to $20, though, they were thinking seriously of contracting to a modest and unassuming D. But whenever Mr. James Dillingham Young came home and reached his flat above he was called "Jim" and greatly hugged by Mrs. James Dillingham Young, already introduced to you as Della. Which is all very good.

-- The Gift of the Magi, O. Henry (1917)

*I*t took her five years to fall in love with the pirate.

It took her another year to decide to tell him.

This was the longest whirlwind romance in the history of time.

Lyric Fielding was waiting, and waiting was something she didn't do well at all. She was a woman of action; a person who liked to get things done. To be *doing*. To be *going*.

Not to be waiting—nerves frayed, pacing the floor—to discover if the man she hadn't seen in nearly a year would show up so she could tell him she loved him.

"And when I put it that way, it sounds insane. Totally nuts," she told Picasso, the big silver-gray cat sunning himself on the windowsill.

Picasso's meow sounded calmly indifferent, the kind of noise that said, "Silly human."

"Well, sure. What does it matter to you? You've been spayed. No more worries about men and whether they show up or not, and how they'll take your completely ridiculous, out-of-the-blue, melodramatic announcement that you love them."

The only response she got to *that* crazy statement was the tiny noise that told her the cat had resumed washing his face with one delicate paw.

She should work. She was well into her latest painting and was planning it to be a gallery piece. The colors and light and images had come to her in a flash of revelation when she was grinding the amethyst to make her paint. Paintings didn't usually appear to her all of a piece like that. She had to coax them out; seduce and tantalize her Muse into coyly revealing a corner here and images there, or maybe giving her a hint as to the theme.

But this one—this one had come to her all at once. It was a seascape, but not a beach scene. Not a calm, happy, 'looking out at the water on a sunny day' painting or a sunset—well, a *sunrise*, since she was in St. Augustine, Florida, and the sun still only rose in the east, as far as she knew. The arrival of vampires and shape shifters and even Atlantis into the world hadn't yet changed *that*.

No, this seascape was different. It contained a man. A tall, dark, and edgy man. All lines and angles; command and presence. On a ship. Standing at the bow, looking off across the waves toward the sunset.

No Freudian messages there, right?

She sighed. Where *was* he?

The painting was all about freedom and adventure and barely leashed power. Things she knew little about. Well, freedom she had. Somewhat. Blindness was not a handicap. It was a disability that she'd learned to manage over the past eighteen years. It was a difference. Not a less-than.

Not a defect.

Just a difference, and everyone had differences.

Okay, she wasn't adventurous either. She was a homebody, and had stayed in her little town of St. Augustine ever since she'd moved in with Aunt Jean after the accident that took her sight and her parents.

She'd spent so many vacations and summers with Jean as a young girl that she could still envision everything about it: the brilliant sun shining down on white-capped waves. The Spanish-inspired buildings. The old fort, which had defended the city in centuries past and now served as a training grounds for soldiers again.

The colors. Everywhere, the colors. The greenest green, the bluest blue. From azure to cerulean, from turquoise to ultramarine. Cobalt to emerald to cadmium blue. All the infinite shades of the sky and ocean in different seasons, at different times of day. Her fingers itched for her paints. Her power shone through her brushstrokes, and she would not trade it for a king's riches.

Her painting, though. *This* painting. All power and movement and the man's fierce, commanding presence. It was Dare; of course it was Dare. Her Atlantean pirate who made her want to be adventurous and free.

Her pirate? Maybe. If she could, just once, be very, very lucky and find her own Christmas miracle.

The bell over the door jingled and she turned at once, but before she blurted out his name, the scent of lilac perfume told her it wasn't him.

"Oh. Hi, Meredith."

Meredith McMasters, Lyric's friend and assistant, started to laugh. "Nice. Has anyone ever been less excited for me to visit in the history of time? No, I think not."

She was acting like a silly school girl, but it made her smile. "I'm sorry. I'm just—"

"Distracted? Preoccupied? Losing your mind waiting for your Atlantean hottie to arrive?"

"All of the above, I guess," she admitted. "I don't know why, even. He said he *might* be here today. It wasn't a guarantee—it wasn't a date. I've just—" She hesitated, but then blurted, "I've just had this terrible feeling all day, scratching at the edge of my mind, that something is wrong. That something is wrong with *him*."

"How would you know?" Meredith, the five-foot-nothing ball of pragmatism disguised as her best friend, pointed out. "He doesn't even have a phone, you said."

"I know. I know." She blew out a breath and resumed pacing back and forth. "Look. It's just that . . . it's just that today was going to be the day."

"The day? Oh. The *day*. Oh, wow. And he hasn't even shown up?"

Lyric paced the carefully measured length of her small studio, wondering whether she should go in the back to her tiny apartment and make some tea.

Drink a shot of whiskey.

Or order some mail-order Valium—was that a thing? It should be a thing.

"It's not even ... it's not even that I expect him to say it back. It's just that after six years, I feel like I need to tell him. Need to find out. Be able to move on."

Meredith's footsteps drew near and then she took one of Lyric's hands in both of hers. "He's a fool if he doesn't love you back, and nobody needs a fool. So either way, you'll be better off once you know."

"I know. You're right. You're always right," Lyric admitted, sighing.

"So smart of you to realize it." With a quick squeeze, Meredith let go of Lyric's hand. "Well, whatever is stressing you out, I can see you've been cleaning. It looks amazing in here. When the tourists show up, I predict a sellout in minutes."

The studio and tiny attached gallery were Lyric's pride and joy. Luckily for her, Aunt Jean had never subscribed to the theory that you can't make a living in the arts. She'd encouraged Lyric's talent for drawing and then painting, buying easels and colored pencils and paper and paints for her, going to art shows, driving her to special classes.

It had started with art therapy. A way for Lyric to cope with her loss. Aunt Jean was a big fan of coping and therapy. But it had become so much more. The first time Lyric put her hands in clay; the first time she put charcoal pencil to paper, she knew she'd found something that would give her the world. She hadn't been blind since birth. The car accident had taken her eyes as well as her family. So she knew color and shadows and light, and she could see the world in her memory and imagination.

All it had taken was for her to build up the confidence to realize that she could draw what was in her mind without seeing the canvas. And then the surprise of learning about the insurance money from the accident that Jean had carefully invested for years, just waiting for Lyric to need it.

She'd found the studio with its tiny attached apartment. She'd been ready, and had the money, thanks to her aunt's careful stewardship. She had independence, and she guarded it fiercely.

As for the painting, well, she remembered a lot. She imagined more. And, after all, she wasn't one hundred percent blind. There were glimmers of light sometimes. And lately—for the past six years, in fact—there'd been something else.

Something *more*.

She'd noticed it the first time she'd had the insane idea to grind up a gemstone into her paint. It didn't make sense. It was a gimmick, her painter friends told her. But it hadn't been a gimmick at all. It'd been a kind of pathway to taking one more step up the ladder toward the ultimate expression of her talent. Something about the gemstones actually helped her envision the colors of the images she wanted to create.

And there was more. More that she'd never told anyone, not even Meredith, who would understand, or Jean, who wouldn't but would pretend to.

When she sang—sang to the gemstones—she somehow felt that the tiny bit of vision she had left was enhanced. That light was brighter and filled more of her visual field.

She could almost *see* colors. Certainly, she could imagine them in her mind more vividly than she'd been able to see them since the accident.

It didn't make sense. She knew it didn't make sense. But what made sense didn't always matter. What made sense was sometimes a barrier to art.

And barriers were only something to break through. Go around, go through, or jump over. She'd learned that lesson the hard way eighteen years ago, and it wasn't one she was about to forget.

But the barrier of vastly different cultures that stood between her and the Atlantean man she'd fallen in love with? The one who called himself a pirate and said he was no good?

Was that a barrier she could cross? Was that a barrier she *should* cross?

She's been asking herself the same questions for the past year, with no better luck at finding answers than she was having right now.

Meredith, who'd been setting up Lyric's paints and humming a Christmas carol to herself, finished the task and brushed her hands off on her pants. The sound shook Lyric out of her mental reverie, and she crossed the six steps to her right until she reached the counter. She picked up the plateful of hot steaming goodness and held it up toward her friend.

"You may have noticed that I made gingerbread cookies for you?"

"I was trying to ignore them. You're killing me. I swear I gain twenty pounds every Christmas just from your baking," Meredith groaned. "And the enormous amount of work that goes into it..."

When Meredith's voice trailed off, Lyric shook her head.

Baking just took more preparation and attention to detail when you were blind. It wasn't *impossible*. She tried to bite back the annoyance she felt at the unspoken "...since you're blind." Meredith was her friend.

But, still. Lyric put the plate back on the counter. "If you don't want any..."

"*Gimme.*"

Better. Lyric took a deep breath. She was on edge because of Dare and everything that hinged on this visit. Not because of anything Meredith might or might not have been planning to say. *Let it go, let it go. Calm, peace, serenity, sugary gingery goodness.*

They sat on stools at the counter, drinking coffee and eating cookies, and talked about everything and nothing, deliberately dancing around the only subject that held center stage in Lyric's mind.

Where was he? Was he okay?

Would he even come – would he ever come again?

It wasn't like she could email sexypirate@Atlantis.com and get an answer.

"He never even gave me a phone number."

"I know. That's just wrong. Are you sure he's not married? The no-phone-number thing is a big red flag to me," Meredith grumbled.

No. He wasn't married. She didn't know how she knew, but she knew that much. He would have told her. Six years, after all.

"It hasn't been that long since Atlantis came up from beneath the sea," Lyric reminded her friend. "It's not like they had cell phone service available down there."

"I know, I know. But it's time for him to get one now," Meredith pointed out, while taking another cookie. "'Can you hear me now' and all that."

"Well, maybe it's no good to him. After all, he's a ship captain. Maybe there's no service in the middle of the ocean. How would I know?" Her stomach started to ache, and she strained to hear something—anything—that might tell her he was coming. The bells on the door, the sound of his boots striking the sidewalk outside the gallery, somebody yelling *Avast, me hearties...*

She was totally losing it.

"They did have Wi-Fi on the cruise I took," Meredith said.

"I don't really get the feeling his ship is a cruise ship. It's more like a cargo ship. He transports things." Cargo ship. *Ha.* He was a pirate. He'd told her often enough, usually in a harsh tone with an edge of bitterness. She should stay away from him. She should. But...why did a tingling sensation feather across her skin, seductive and enticing, at the mere thought of him? Why did she feel hot and cold and giddy and dreamy and as if her skin cells each individually became electrified whenever he was near?

She suddenly realized Meredith was talking to her and wrenched her mind out of its ever-so-deliciously arousing reverie and back to the conversation at hand.

"Aha. Listen. You already told me, that night we went out for cactus margaritas, that the man calls himself a pirate. He doesn't even have a last name, or so he claims. I don't think this is the kind of guy you need to get involved with, whether he shows up or not. Whether he says he loves you or not. It scares me." The words were accompanied by a deep sigh.

Lyric could hear the sincerity in the troubled sound of her friend's voice. She nodded, but then shook her head. "No. I've been talking to him for six years. Granted, only a few times a year, and then only for a few hours at a time. But he's not secretly married. He's not hiding something evil. He's not a criminal. He's ... special. Kind of funny and brilliant and—"

"I know, I know. He's all that and a bag of chips," Meredith said, resignation clear in her tone. "I hope he shows up. I really do. Do you want me to stay?"

"No ... no. I'm fine. You got all the new paints set out?"

"All set out in the proper order," Meredith confirmed. "We didn't get the yellow ochre that you wanted, but it's supposed to come in next week. Hey, I gotta run. Things to do, yada yada."

"Why don't you take some cookies with you? Take lots."

Meredith laughed. "But my ass will never fit in my jeans again if I eat one more cookie. You keep them. I bet pirates love gingerbread cookies."

She leaned in and gave Lyric a quick hug, and then headed out, the sound of whistling accompanying her footsteps as she went. Meredith was someone who always lived in the moment, and sometimes Lyric wished she could be more like her friend.

She stood, taking a cookie and biting into the warm, gingery goodness, and took the twelve steps from the counter toward her easel. The painting was nearly finished. She'd had thoughts the night before about what she might do next, and thinking about it carried over into her dreams, which wasn't all that unusual for her. She dreamed of bright vibrant colors, as if the moonlight gave wings to her imagination and offered her the gift of what the day had stolen from her.

Almost Christmas. She'd had to smile and evade with so many people. She had an amazing group of friends whom she loved and who loved her. She'd received a multitude of invitations to spend Christmas with this family or that; with this couple or that group of singles. She would have no lack of choice for where to eat her Christmas goose, if anybody even ate Christmas goose anymore outside of the Dickens tale. But she hadn't wanted to commit to anything because she had The Plan.

The Plan had two steps: Tell Dare she loved him, and invite him to stay with her for Christmas. What could be simpler?

She moaned and smacked her forehead with her hand. What could be simpler? Ha. What could be more impossibly dangerous to her self-esteem?

Or her heart?

But six years...it was time to paint or put away her brushes.

Christmas was her favorite time of the year. It had been the week before Christmas six years ago when she'd first met Dare. He'd barged into her studio, larger than life, blocking what little light glimmered at the edges of her awareness and taking up more psychic space than was possible, as if he defied the laws of physics themselves. He'd been rude, arrogant, and fascinating.

"Are you the artist? And what kind of name is Lyric for an artist? You should be a musician with that name." The growl of the voice that asked the question was rich and deep, like honey poured over melted chocolate. A tiny shiver went up Lyric's spine at the sound, and she turned toward the visitor, paint brush in hand.

"No, I'm the cobbler," she said brightly. *"Do you need shoes?"*

He laughed, but she could hear the note of surprise in his laughter. Maybe he wasn't a man who found much humor in life.

"Point to you. You're the painter, I'm the pirate. I've got your gemstones. Do you have my money?"

"I have your money. If you're a pirate, what are you doing on

land? Do you have the habit of making all your deliveries personally? Even I have an assistant. Maybe you're not a very good
pirate."

She brushed her hands off on her skirt and then put them in
her pockets to hide the fact that they were trembling a little. She
didn't know why, but she instinctively knew she didn't want him
to see it. She needed a strong front with this one, she could tell
already.

She walked over to the counter and reached underneath for
her purse. "How many gemstones, what kind, and what do you
want for them?"

She raised her face to look in the direction of where she sensed
his was and ignored his sharp inhalation.

He'd just figured out she was blind. They all took a moment
or two to get used to the idea.

She waited for the questions, sighing a little to herself. Here
we go.

How can a blind person be an artist? A painter?

Or the false flattery—the condescension. Oh, what a nice
painting you have there. ("For a blind person" was always
implied, if not outright stated.)

She wasn't some kind of trained monkey or an oddity for
people to stare at. She turned down any media requests that held
the slightest hint of being about how good she was—for a
woman painter. How good she was for a blind painter.

She just wanted to be a good painter. Period.

"So, I have a question," he said.

Lyric took a deep breath and steeled herself for the stupidity,
knowing it would ruin the incipient fantasy she had going about
him just from the sound of his voice.

"Is that a cat, or a footstool with feet?"

She laughed a little bit at the memory. He'd caught her
off guard and made her laugh then, too. Made her smile.

Made her want to talk to him. They'd talked for hours, and she'd even invited him to dinner, which had been a bold move for her. She was a homebody, and he was a man she'd never met before.

A self-proclaimed pirate.

She'd been exhilarated by her daring—ha. *Daring.* She was making stupid puns now.

But Dare had declined. He'd said he had other engagements to keep. She'd fancied that she heard a little regret in his tone, or so she comforted herself later.

But he came back. He came back the next month, even though she hadn't put in an order with the intermediary for more rare gems. Only gemstones from the Fae lands worked as a catalyst for her paints, and they were very hard to get.

Dare came to visit her, anyway. He brought a few stones, and then a month later, he brought a few more. These were from Atlantis, he'd told her. From his personal collection.

He wouldn't let her pay for them, and he'd told her some crazy story about how she could cause an international incident between Atlantis and the United States if she refused his gift.

She'd been about ninety-nine percent sure he was full of crap, but that one percent had made her stop arguing and accept the gems as graciously as she'd known how to.

And so it went. After a year of sporadic visits, he finally went out to dinner with her.

By the third year, he'd trusted her enough to tell her about Atlantis.

By the fourth year, he'd finally allowed her to touch his face and learn what he looked like from her fingertips—and the sensation of his skin, warm beneath her hands, had gone straight to her soul.

The touch had lingered on the tips of her fingers for months.

By the fifth year, she'd fallen in love with him. This man she'd never even kissed had a claim on her heart. She just didn't know how to tell him, so she didn't. And then...well, then his visits became more sporadic.

He came once every three months or so instead of every month. Also, he seemed increasingly abrupt and on edge. She didn't know why. When she'd asked him, he'd said only that he never signed up to be an ambassador. All the hoopla surrounding Atlantis finally rising from beneath the sea had been hard on all of them, he said, and he was definitely getting his share of problems from the people he usually did business with. They all wanted something from him. Access. Partnerships. Sales channels. Black-market goods from Atlantis.

It was too much, and he was sick to death of it.

"Enough that you'd give up going to sea?" she'd asked him once.

"Never." He'd sounded shocked at the thought. "Being a sea captain isn't only what I do, Lyric. It's who I *am*. Without the sea, I'd be nothing."

A shiver snaked its way through her at the memory. Really, could anything have been a clearer warning to stay away? Without the sea, he'd be nothing. Where was the space for a quiet homebody of an artist in that life?

Her watch chimed out a lilting melody, telling her it was seven o'clock. An hour past time to close. He hadn't come. He wasn't coming. At least not now. Maybe he'd arrive later in the week, or after the new year. She could talk to him then. She could tell him...

Or she could *not* tell him.

She was starting to feel like not telling him might be the wiser choice. She needed to accept that it was time to move on. Time to get thoughts of the honey-voiced Atlantean pirate out of her mind and out of her heart, before she had a chance to fall any further.

"All I need is you, Picasso," she told her large, furry, foot-stool-shaped cat. "Right?"

Picasso arched his back under her hand and purred as she stroked his silky head.

"Time to close up shop." She turned toward the door, but before she even took a first step, it crashed open, bells jangling out a discordant warning.

"I think I need your help," a man groaned. It was Dare; she knew him instantly. She could smell the sharp scent of wind and sky and saltwater that was uniquely his; she could pick his voice out of a thousand others.

"Dare?" She started toward him. "Are you hurt—"

"I think I need—"

A heavy thud was the only conclusion to his sentence. A shudder ran through her, freezing her in place for a moment. He'd collapsed. She rushed over, slamming her knee into the corner of the counter in her haste, but ignoring the pain. She slowed her pace, and when she felt the edge of his body with her foot, she knelt down beside him. She reached for his pulse, her fingers finding their way to the spot. It was there; strong and reassuring. He was soaking wet, though; his skin was icy cold and he was shivering violently.

"Dare? *Dare*? What happened?"

He didn't answer. Maybe he *couldn't* answer. And of course she couldn't see him, so she couldn't even guess how badly he was hurt.

She pulled her phone out of her pocket and told it to call Dr. Miller.

No. She pressed *END CALL.*

"Call 911."

No pirates were going to die on her watch.

3

———

Della finished her cry and attended to her cheeks with the powder rag. She stood by the window and looked out dully at a gray cat walking a gray fence in a gray backyard. Tomorrow would be Christmas Day, and she had only $1.87 with which to buy Jim a present. She had been saving every penny she could for months, with this result. Twenty dollars a week doesn't go far. Expenses had been greater than she had calculated. They always are. Only $1.87 to buy a present for Jim. Her Jim. Many a happy hour she had spent planning for something nice for him. Something fine and rare and sterling—something just a little bit near to being worthy of the honor of being owned by Jim.

-- *The Gift of the Magi*, O. Henry (1917)

Dare was pretty sure he was dead.

Or at least deep beneath the ocean and about to be dead. He tossed and turned, fighting the shards of pain ripping up his head and lungs. Fighting to break through the darkness surrounding him. He had flashes of awareness

—flashes of color and light. And each time, the beautiful face of what must be an angel was right there, looking down at him.

Individual words pierced the haze of his mind. Geometric shapes of language that stabbed him and prodded him with sharp edges, but had no meaning to the chaos in his brain.

His head hurt like it'd never hurt before, and he'd certainly been a victim of many mishaps considering his calling. Life on the high seas wasn't exactly designed for the faint of heart—or the fragile of bone. But this was different. His brains—if he had any left—were surely leaking out his ears.

Someone or something opened his eyelids, and the light from the lamp spiked into his eyes. He tried to remember how to form words, but managed only a harsh grunting noise that he hoped to the nine hells *somebody* recognized as the word *stop*.

The light went away, at least, and they let him close his eyes, but that's when it occurred to him that he might not be dead after all. Unless he was, in fact, caught in the first level of the nine hells; trapped in pain for eternity for a life filled with misdeeds and self-absorption.

A gentle voice that rang with an undertone of silvery bells: "You're going to be fine, Dare. It's only a concussion."

He *knew* that voice.

Lyric.

He reached out instinctively, and her warm, slender hand clasped his. Her touch calmed him, soothed the jagged edges of his mind in a way he knew he had no right to feel, but he'd be damned if he wouldn't take advantage of it for the short time he could do so.

Another voice, this one slightly deeper but still female,

spoke next. "He took a hell of a hit, Lyric. But it's almost as if he's healing right in front of my eyes. If I hadn't seen it, I never would've believed it, and I would insist that you go to the hospital head trauma unit. But he's gone from a major injury to a mild concussion in the space of the last ten minutes."

"Well, the way he fought with the EMTs to not get in that ambulance made it pretty clear that he wasn't in any major trouble. Nobody at death's door would have that much energy," the silvery voice said, still sounding concerned, but with an edge of laughter.

Dare started to sink again then, and after that, only snatches of sentences made it through to his conscious mind.

"... watch him."

"Thank you. I'll ..."

Then the voices faded to unintelligible sounds in the background, and he let himself drift back under, inexplicably reassured that the owner of that silvery voice would keep him safe. He was exactly where he belonged.

"*D*are? I need you to wake up. Can you look at me?"

Lyric. He opened his eyes. Even shadowed by the light of the lamp behind her, he knew her face.

A cloud of riotous black curls surrounded her face and touched her shoulders, and her eyes looked dark in the shadows, but he knew from six years of looking into them that they shone like beautiful copper, a color as rare and precious as the metal in the armband that contained the magic of his spirit bond with Seranth. He started to raise his hand to touch the band, but the movement sent a jolt of painful protest through his muscles, and he winced.

"Dr. Miller told me not to let you sleep too long. She wanted me to keep checking your eyes, but of course we know I can't do that. Can you hold still for a moment while I take a picture to send to the doctor?"

Before he could answer, a light flashed in his eyes, making him flinch. But he'd clearly already improved a great deal, because the light was far less painful than the last time. All credit to superior Atlantean healing powers, of course.

Maybe, though, some credit went to the woman seated at his side. He was too tired to pursue the thought...

The next time Dare woke up, the room was swimming around him. Waves of sensation buffeted him from all sides, but unlike his dive into the ocean, this was a gentler current. He felt like the shore might be in sight. He opened his eyes and realized he was in a bed. In a room.

A room on land; not his berth on the *Luna*.

Lyric.

He remembered calling her name in his mind. Reaching out to her when hope and light and life itself were about to be lost. All he'd wanted was one last look at her face. One last chance to hear the sound of her voice, before the ocean took him into silence and darkness forever It would have been enough.

This was better.

The portal—it must have worked. The room was rimmed with shadow, lit only by a bedside lamp on a small wooden table. He glanced around, curious about this place. A private sanctuary that perhaps held her secrets as much as the mystery in her copper eyes. In six years of knowing her, he'd never once seen her bedroom.

He laughed a little at the thought. The men and women he caroused with regularly at dockside bars would never believe it. Captain Dare of the *Luna*—celibate. Perhaps celibate wasn't the word. It *had* been six years since he met her, and he was a man. But the encounters he'd had with other women since then had been brief and unsatisfactory. For some reason he couldn't understand, after the first time he'd met Lyric, the vision of her eyes, her face, her curls, and even the sound of her voice seemed never far from his mind.

His thinking was still muddled. That last crack on the head had been no joke. At least his crew...wait. His crew. What had happened to them? He tried to reach out on the Atlantean mental pathway to reach someone—anyone— who might have heard what had happened to his ship and crew. None on board were Atlantean, so he had no way to reach them directly.

His brain flinched from the attempt, though, and he heard nothing in return. Perhaps he was too far away or too injured. He'd try again as soon as his head quit pounding quite so much.

And the unicorns—Bingley and Jane. By Poseidon, he hoped they had survived. If he'd caused the world to lose two such magnificent creatures, he'd never forgive himself. If he ever told her about it, Lyric probably wouldn't forgive him, either.

Lyric. His mind kept wandering off from the most important question. Where was she? He tried to sit up but fell back against the pillows, weaker than he'd realized.

"Lyric," he croaked out of his damaged throat. "Water."

Just then, perhaps in response to his raspy call, Lyric appeared in the doorway with a bottle of water in one hand and that infernal camera device in the other.

"Water," he repeated, holding out a hand.

She stopped in the doorway, her wide eyes turned toward him. A smile like the sun rising over the horizon on a clear day spread across her face.

"You're awake. You're talking," she said unnecessarily. He already knew both of those things.

"Water."

She walked the six paces to the bed, uncapping the bottle of water as she came. "Here you go. But just sips, please. Dr. Miller said to give you a little at a time so you didn't bring it all right back up."

He tried to raise his head, but before he could put any real effort into it, her hand slid under his neck and supported him so he could drink. Dare closed his eyes at the sheer bliss of the water sliding down his throat and her cool hand on his head. He tried to be a gentlemen and not notice how close her delightfully round breasts were to his face, but gave it up as a lost cause.

After all, he wasn't a gentleman—he was a pirate. And the sight of her curvy body was a wonderful prize for a man who'd thought he'd never see her again. Six years of meetings—of waiting for the chance to see her again. To talk to her, make her laugh, watch her slightly unfocused copper eyes sparkle with amusement. To inhale the delicate scent of flowers and the stronger aroma of charcoal and paint that surrounded her. To watch her graceful movements.

Imagine her touch on his skin, her taste in his mouth.

Six years of being beguiled by her kindness and humor and intelligence. Six years of being tempted by her luscious body. The curve of her cheek. The way her gleaming hair fell around her face in the sunlight. How much his hands ached to reach out and grasp her amazing ass and pull him toward her, inch by tantalizing inch.

Naked.

He closed his eyes and groaned, shifting his body to try to get comfortable. At least she couldn't see the erection that was straining the fabric of his pants.

"Oh, no," she said, probably thinking he was groaning in pain. Well, it *was* pain, just a different kind. "How are you feeling? I should take another picture of your eyes for—"

"No," he said firmly, wincing at the thought. "I have definitely had enough of that damn flashing light in my eyes. I'm fine. Superior Atlantean healing."

Lyric sat down in a chair that was pulled up next to the bed. She must've been sitting there next to him for hours, because every memory of the night that was coming back to him contained the image of her face.

He struggled to sit up, letting her help him just for the opportunity to breathe in her scent. Then he tried to swallow, in spite of the painful lump suddenly blocking his throat. "I'm sorry. I shouldn't have brought my problems to your doorstep. I didn't have–" He stopped just short of admitting there hadn't been anywhere else he'd rather go. His confession seemed at once too much and yet not enough. It'd taken him five minutes to become fascinated with this woman, and then he'd spent the next five years—no, six, now—fighting his attraction. She was human. She was an artist. She was a self-professed homebody.

The last thing she needed in her life was a pirate of poor reputation and worse deeds.

He watched, fascinated, as her cheeks turned pink, and then her graceful hands reached for the bottle of water.

"I'm glad you did. Here, drink a little more. Are you hungry? No, you're probably not hungry. Dr. Wilson said the head injury would make you nauseous for a while. But when you're ready, I can make you some soup. I have half a roasted chicken I could put in with some carrots, and maybe

I could find some onion and a little—" She broke off, biting her lip, her cheeks flushing again. "I'm sorry I'm babbling. I have to admit I've been worried sick about you. I wanted you to go to the emergency room, but you quite strenuously refused."

Abruptly, he remembered a chaotic moment of battling someone who was trying to hold him down. Suddenly alarmed, he looked up at her. If he'd harmed her in any way, he'd never forgive himself. "I didn't hurt you, did I? Or anybody else?"

She shook her head. "No. You were quite gentle with me. And it's not like the EMTs don't have experience dealing with unruly patients. They were quite competent at restraining you in order to secure vitals. Between the three of them," she added ruefully. "Luckily, my neighbor Dr. Miller—Penny—was walking her Goldendoodle, so she came in to have a look. She said she'd be glad to keep an eye out for you if I was definitely sure that I wasn't going to send you to the ER in restraints."

Dare scowled. "I have no good experience with restraints. It is well for them that they stopped when they did. Even half-conscious, I could well have hurt someone."

"Yeah, we kinda got that," she said dryly. "Superior Atlantean strength, huh?"

He took another long drink of water, but then could feel himself slipping back under. He was so tired. So very tired, as if he hadn't slept in weeks instead of only days. The trip had been a rough one, and he'd only caught catnaps in his cabin a few times. He felt like he could sleep for a week.

But only if he could stay here. With her. In her home, her room, her bed.

Her arms.

If only she'd allow him to hold her. Longing slammed

into him, tightening his chest, and he pinned his gaze to her expressive face. How could eyes that couldn't see still say so much? "I can stay, can't I? Just until I feel better? I would not wish to be a burden upon you, but—"

A wave of heat smashed into him, and he made a grunting sound at the pain that started hammering his skull. "Sorry. My head. I was saying--"

His forgot what he'd meant to say. He was trapped in a sudden typhoon of swirling, cascading heat, and his mind went hazy. Fever. Or worse?

"Shh." She rested a gentle hand on his forehead, and he closed his eyes in relief at her cool touch. "Of course you can stay, Dare. Don't worry about anything. I'll take care of you, and what I don't – or can't – do, Meredith or Dr. Miller will help me with."

Every muscle in his body relaxed at her promise. "So tired," he mumbled. "So very tired."

"Sleep, then. Sleep, and I'll watch over you."

He drifted off on currents of tropically warm water and the surprised realization that she was singing to him. It was French, he knew that much. He'd been to Paris a few times. He'd even been to Avignon and seen the bridge in her song. And he'd so love to dance with her there. She'd be so incredibly beautiful, with French lavender in her hair...He could feel himself floating away again, lulled by the silvery notes of her song and the vision of dancing with her.

"*Sur le pont D'Avignon, On y danse, On y danse...*"

"So beautiful." Had he said it or merely thought it? He wasn't sure. It didn't seem to matter.

She touched his face and spoke again, so softly that he almost didn't hear. "Oh, Dare. I was just thinking the same thing about you."

4

There was a pier-glass between the windows of the room. *Perhaps you have seen a pier-glass in an $8 flat. A very thin and very agile person may, by observing his reflection in a rapid sequence of longitudinal strips, obtain a fairly accurate conception of his looks. Della, being slender, had mastered the art.*

Suddenly she whirled from the window and stood before the glass. Her eyes were shining brilliantly, but her face had lost its color within twenty seconds. Rapidly she pulled down her hair and let it fall to its full length.

-- *The Gift of the Magi*, O. Henry (1917)

Lyric didn't know whether to laugh or cry. Emotions were bubbling up inside of her—so many emotions that she didn't know how to handle them. Couldn't recognize them; couldn't identify them. Didn't know how to cope. Her breath was too fast, too shallow, and she was shivering with reaction from the morning's adrenaline letdown from the night's fear.

She'd been terrified when he'd arrived feeling so icy cold, like he was near death, and that fear hadn't quite subsided over the hours she'd spent watching over him. She still didn't know what had happened. He'd raved and ranted about a storm, Poseidon, and unicorns, of all things. She chalked it up to the head injury. No doubt he would tell her the true story when he was feeling a little better. In the meantime, she'd sit right back in the chair where she'd already spent hours listening to him breathe, holding his hand while he slept, and sending prayers that he would survive and be okay.

Even while he slept, his presence filled her small bedroom, electric and larger than life. He radiated an energy that called to her, sent a frisson of awareness down her spine that tingled and lifted the hairs on the back of her neck .

Awareness of *him*.

He was sleeping again, and this time she hoped it was restful. His forehead felt warm, but maybe that was just the aftereffect of being wounded? The "superior" Atlantean healing at work raising his metabolism? She didn't know, and it wasn't like she could Google it.

But he *was* resting this time, not tossing and turning and muttering as he'd been doing before.

Lyric was so tempted to touch him again, but this time, finally, more than just his face. To explore him with her fingertips. To measure the breath of his shoulders, the muscles in his arms and chest, and even to stroke his hair. When she lifted his head to drink, she'd been able to run her fingers through the thick waves of his hair, which was something she'd been longing to do for a long time.

She slid forward to the edge of her seat, tried to speak,

and then cleared her throat and tried again. "Dare? Dare, are you awake? Would you mind if I touch you?"

He didn't answer, so she decided to take that as permission, in spite of the fact that she'd deliberately whispered. Which was completely and entirely wicked of her, but she couldn't resist the temptation. Six long *years* of temptation.

She was tired of trying.

She reached out with both hands, tentatively at first, until she touched the firm curve of his shoulder, and then less so. Her fingers shaped the edges of him—the edges of a man. He was all hard muscle. Strength and sinew wrapped around his shoulders, arms, and chest like armbands. There was no give to him—no yielding.

Who could live with such a hard man? Who would want to? She already knew the answer to the latter, but was still unsure about the former. She knew him; had grown to know so much of his heart during their time together over the years. She knew his kindness but she also knew his hard edges. A pirate, perhaps—a warrior, definitely. Was he the right match for her? Doubts stirred, but she squashed them. She deserved a chance to find out.

He mumbled something. A name. Seranth. A twinge of something that felt a lot like jealousy curled up from her throat, but then subsided. He'd told her about Seranth and explained their bond. Seranth was a sea spirit; a water elemental, and they worked in tandem to sail his ship, the *Luna*, across the seas. Seranth was part of him. She was also part of the ship itself, and part of the sea and sky. He'd said he couldn't describe it any more clearly than that, but that had been enough for Lyric. She'd told him she thought she understood, at least a little.

She herself had felt the presence of a guardian angel in her life ever since the night of the car crash that took her parents. An angel whose serene and protective presence had been with her ever since. It was different, but a little bit the same. Angel and spirit. Christian and pagan. Dare came from a time before Christ, and she lived in Christ's grace. But she knew—hoped—that what was between them could transcend differences and bridge barriers. She prayed that he would recover, and then she would admit her feelings to him. She would invite him to stay with her for Christmas and celebrate the holidays with her family and friends.

Maybe he'd even invite her to Atlantis sometime.

He stirred beneath her fingertips, and she realized she'd been stroking his hair for several minutes without even realizing what she was doing. She felt his forehead again with the back of her hand out of habit, not at all expecting the blazing heat in his skin. She snatched her hand away, shocked. He should be *glowing* at that temperature. She had to call Penny. Something was seriously wrong—surely this couldn't just be his metabolism.

It had to be fever, or maybe something worse. *Please God* let it not be something worse.

She started to rise to retrieve her phone from the kitchen, but his hand shot out and grasped her wrist with unbreakable strength.

"Don't leave me," he demanded. For demand it was. Sick or no, he wasn't asking; he was telling. This was the voice of a sea captain in complete control.

"I need to call the doctor, Dare. I need to—"

He yanked on her arm so she fell forward onto the bed and partially on top of him. Before she could move, he curved one of those strong arms around her and held tight.

"No. Stay with me. I need you. *Please.*"

This time, his voice was less demand and more seduction. Silken tones from his damaged throat—honey over whiskey. Playful, but implacable.

"I need you to hold me, Lyric. Beautiful Lyric. Six long years of wanting to hold you, and it only took almost dying," he murmured into her hair.

She froze, unable to believe what he was saying. Unable to believe that he was saying the exact things she herself had felt for so long.

Oh, oh, oh, oh. He smelled like salt and sea and sky and *man*. Delicious, unbelievably sexy man. She closed her eyes, snuggled into the curve of his embrace, and took a deep, happy breath.

But then she shook her head and told herself to snap out of it.

"Dare. I can't—we need to—you're burning up. I have to call the doctor. You probably have an infection from where your head was sliced open. I don't really know how 'superior Atlantean healing powers' work on infection, so I'm gonna propose we go with good, old-fashioned human antibiotics."

"I'm fine," he muttered into her hair. "Don't need anything but you."

She inhaled sharply, whether from shock, surprise, or a massive case of untimely lust, she didn't know. What she was feeling wasn't important, though, no matter how much she'd wanted to hear exactly that from him. What *mattered* was that she get him some medicine.

"Okay. You need to let me go. Now," she said, injecting a firm tone into her voice. It was the voice she used with young art students. No-nonsense. In charge. They always snapped to attention immediately.

Teacher voice had absolutely zero effect on Dare.

His response instead was to tighten his arms around her

and start kissing her neck. An electric sensation shot straight to every erotic part of her body from the spot she hadn't realized was so exquisitely sensitive until his lips caressed it, and she really thought she might either melt or go up in flames.

"Dare! Listen—"

He gently bit her earlobe.

"*Ohhhhh*," she moaned, before she could help it. "No. Dare! Not now. I need to get you some antibiotics."

He pulled his head away from her neck, and she took a moment to sincerely regret it. Before she could say anything else, though, he put his hand on her butt.

This time it was he who moaned. Or groaned. A sound from deep in his throat that rumbled in his chest beneath her cheek, and made her want to rip his shirt off with her teeth. "Oh, Lyric. Oh, *Lyric.*"

"I—what?"

"You have the nicest, roundest ass I've ever seen," he told her with all evidence of true appreciation.

She blinked and tried to push up and away from him, but one arm tightened around her, while the other hand continued to caress her bottom, causing her thighs to clench against the rush of liquid heat flaming through her entire body.

"Thanks a *lot*," she said somewhat tartly. "Just what every woman wants to hear—that her butt is big. Any other compliments you want to throw my way?"

"Perfect, just like the rest of you. You're so hot. So lush. So *delicious*. And when I finally sink into you, I bet you'll be so wet for me. So, so wet and hot." His voice was a rasp of sex and seduction that was slowly driving her completely insane by mirroring the rough pleasure thrilling through her at his possessive embrace, and the heat was building between her thighs as if his words had been a premonition.

"I've wanted to get my hands on your ass for years," he said, his hand tightening on that overly sensitized part of her body. His other hand stroked up the side of her body until it rested on the side of her breast. "And your breasts. Oh, your *breasts*. I think poets could write songs to your breasts. I need you, Lyric. I *need* you."

She gasped, unable to form words, to deny him, even to think in the rush of heat and feeling and pure, primal pleasure throbbing through her.

He released her breast and threaded the fingers of his hand through her hair to cup her head. "Let me put my mouth on you."

Lyric went boneless; every synapse she had shot fireworks through her nerve cells—through her veins—even through her bones. She'd never been so indescribably, overwhelmingly, incandescently aroused in her life.

Naturally, her freaking conscience decided to speak up and tell her that she was in imminent danger of hooking up with an Atlantean who was addled by injury and fever. Not exactly the best way to start off a relationship.

Freaking conscience.

She sighed.

"Dare. Enough. You're burning up. Let me get you some antibiotics. A big, fat needle filled with penicillin might take your mind off your libido—"

"Your ass," he mumbled dreamily, and she could feel him smile against her neck.

"And off my ass," she agreed, sighing.

"Kiss me."

"What?" Surely he hadn't said...

"Kiss me, and I'll let you go get needles and pessanillin.

Pennalissen. Parasillin. Whatever."

"Deal," she said, before she could have second thoughts about taking total advantage of an injured, delirious man. He had his hands on her ass, after all.

"Deal. Now. And on my lips," he said firmly. "No cheating with forehead kissing."

Lyric took a deep breath. She needed to steel herself for this, in spite of—or perhaps because—she'd wanted it for so long.

"Okay, you can kiss me now."

He laughed. "No, my copper-eyed beauty. You have to kiss *me.*"

She summoned her nerve and pulled away from him a little bit; just enough to raise her head so she could reach his lips with her own.

Her brain and all parts much farther south were doing cartwheels at the idea that she was planning to *kiss Dare*, so she told them to calm the heck down. This was going to be a chaste, calming, gentle kiss with a closed mouth, offered just so he'd let her go get medicine for him.

She took a deep breath, and then she leaned forward and reached toward the sound of his voice with her fingertips. When she found his mouth, she traced it for a moment, finding it firm and unsmiling, his lips softening at her touch. She took another breath, as if preparing to dive into dangerous waters, and touched her lips to his.

And the world turned upside down.

The moment her lips met his, Dare tightened his arms on her and half-sat, half -rolled, until he had her beneath him, and then he took total control over what she'd laughingly—ridiculously—thought was a kiss. That wasn't a kiss.

This was a kiss.

He didn't take; he plundered. He teased and seduced;

advanced and retreated. He kissed her with skill and hunger and that sense of barely leashed power that made her head spin. She slipped her arms around him and kissed him back, meeting him beat for beat, breath for breath.

She wondered, gloried, reveled in the feel of his hard body against hers and the taste of salt and spice of his mouth.

This was a *kiss*—and she dimly realized that, once it ended, she would never, ever be the same.

She kissed him, surrendering and conquering, advancing and retreating herself, because she was unable to do anything else. She took his mouth with passion and heat and hunger, and he responded in kind. For long moments, maybe hours, maybe an eternity, she knew nothing but his fever-hot skin and strength and demand.

Fever-hot skin...wait. Fever...

She had to stop. He needed help.

She pulled away, panting, shuddering in an attempt to draw breath while emerging from the punch-drunk sense of complete and utter desire.

"Dare. I can't--"

"You can. You *will*," he commanded, pulling her head closer. "Mine. Now."

She moaned, but forced herself to turn her head, escaping his kiss that she wanted so badly.

When she forced herself to pull away, they were both breathing hard, and his skin temperature was in the fiery blaze range. *Damn*. She'd forgotten her end goal somehow during that explosion of feeling.

"Dare," she said, still breathing hard. " I need to get you that medicine."

He instantly released her. "A deal is a deal, I always tell Seranth...*Seranth*? Seranth?"

Lyric sat up and then swung her feet off the bed to stand, but he seemed to have forgotten all about her.

"My armband! Where is it? Did you take it off? Did that doctor...*Seranth?*" He was shouting by the end, the anguish clear.

She knew what the sea spirit meant to him, and a bolt of pain clenched her chest at his loss. "No. We didn't take it, Dare. You didn't have it on when you arrived. Your shirt was torn...is it possible that it fell off in the water?"

She reached out to touch his shoulder, but he brushed her hand off and pushed himself up to a sitting position.

"No. It can't fall off. It's not jewelry; it's the physical manifestation of my bond with Seranth. Poseidon bestowed it, and only he..." His voice trailed off and then she jumped at the sound of his fist crashing into the end table.

"He took it. He took her away from me."

The pain in his voice buffeted her, and she flinched away. She'd never heard a human voice filled with such suffering since...since the accident. Her mother hadn't died right away, and Lyric had heard—no. *No.* She forcibly locked that memory away. There was a man who needed her right here in the present.

"Dare. I can't—what can I do? How can I help? I'll call the doctor to come over and see—"

Before she could finish her sentence, he lurched up off the bed, stumbled into her, and knocked them both to the floor. He'd somehow rolled over in mid-fall, so his back and head took the brunt of the impact, but it was still enough to knock the air out of her for a minute .

When she could stop gasping, she sat up and turned to him. "Dare? Are you okay?"

But his body lay still, unmoving beside her, and her only answer was silence.

Now, there were two possessions of the James Dillingham Youngs in which they both took a mighty pride. One was Jim's gold watch that had been his father's and his grandfather's. The other was Della's hair. Had the queen of Sheba lived in the flat across the airshaft, Della would have let her hair hang out the window some day to dry just to depreciate Her Majesty's jewels and gifts. Had King Solomon been the janitor, with all his treasures piled up in the basement, Jim would have pulled out his watch every time he passed, just to see him pluck at his beard from envy.

-- The Gift of the Magi, O. Henry (1917)

"Welcome to Atlantis!"

Dare watched Lyric as she stood, frozen, in the middle of the palace garden. She was holding her small blue book she called a passport in one hand and a travel bag in the other. He was carrying her larger case; the one that contained her paints and brushes and a few small canvases that she'd refused to leave without.

"I can't—I can't believe I'm here. I thought... I thought we had to go find a train, or plane tickets, or a boat—" she paused, a stricken expression on her face. "I'm sorry, Dare. I didn't mean to—I know you need to go find out what happened to your ship. You can just drop me somewhere and go do what you need to do."

He didn't bother to say that he'd already been doing exactly that, reaching out on the shared Atlantean mental pathway to anyone who knew anything about his ship. One of the portal guards had responded very briefly, so at least Dare knew his ship, his crew, and Bingley and Jane were safe, if nothing else.

"It's fine. Everyone is fine and safe. I can go check on the ship later. First let's get you—" His voice trailed off at the sight of Lyric, standing, chin raised, body held stiffly upright, reminded him of the courage it must have taken her to trust him. To travel through the portal. To actually come to Atlantis, so far in so many ways from her tiny home in her tiny town. She was amazing. It was her first trip *anywhere*, she'd told him, and it was to *Atlantis*. The land long thought to be myth by her kind. And yet her first thought was for him and his ship and crew. How long had it been since he'd known such selfless caring?

Too long to remember.

It had been the same way all throughout the night, while he'd tossed and turned with fever from a budding infection. He had vague memories of kissing her, holding her in his arms and—surely not?—having his hands on her lovely ass. Then strange memories intruded, of needles pricking him in the arm, and the fever finally subsided. When he'd awoken this morning, it had been to the lovely sound of her singing, which he'd wanted to keep listening to. So he'd pretended he was still asleep and lay there in her bed, with her scent of peach and vanilla and spice surrounding him, and listened to the song of the woman it'd taken him five years to realize he'd fallen in love with.

Luckily for her, he was never, ever going to tell her that. When you lived a life characterized by a bad reputation that you absolutely deserved, you knew better than to think your darkness had a chance at finding love with someone so wholly of the light.

But in spite of everything, he'd wanted her near him. By the time he'd finally let her know that he was awake, he'd come up with a plan. And his first words had been *Come to Atlantis with me.*

She'd sat there in the chair beside the bed, shock on her lovely face, those gorgeous copper eyes wide and slightly unfocused. He forgot sometimes that she was blind because she was so completely in command of herself and the space in her studio. Even on the few occasions that they'd ventured out to local restaurants together, she'd been capable and perfectly independent. He realized it was ridiculous to think she might be otherwise. The loss of one sense didn't mean the loss of all, or the diminishing of intelligence. And clearly, she'd found ways to compensate for that loss.

So he'd asked again. "Will you come to Atlantis with me?"

She'd taken a deep breath and said yes, surprising them both.

While he'd cleaned up and gotten dressed, he'd heard a flurry of activity going on out in her studio. Lyric's friend Meredith had come by and packed up Lyric's paints for her in a very precise order, and also took the cat home with her for the holidays.

Holidays. This was something new for him, too. Atlantis

would be celebrating its first Christmas, thanks to King Conlan's human, Christian wife. There'd been a frenzy of decorating and baking going on when Dare had last left port, but he'd ignored it because it was annoying. Someone was always getting in his way or underfoot, even his brother Liam, who generally operated on the same isolationist policy toward family that Dare had. Suddenly Liam was cornering him and inviting him to "family" meals with his new wife, Jaime.

He'd avoided them as much as possible and was relieved, in a slightly guilty way, that Liam and Jaime would be traveling out of Atlantis for the next week or so. The last thing he needed was to overwhelm Lyric with his family, when he knew that she could never become part of it. She deserved better than him and his screwed-up relatives.

All of this went through his head in seconds. He turned toward Lyric and saw that she'd put her bag down on the ground and was reaching out to touch the flowering bush nearest her. It sported huge masses of yellow and purple blooms, and he'd never seen a similar plant outside of Atlantis.

"Oh, Dare, this scent. The scent of these flowers is the most amazing thing I've ever smelled. I feel like I could almost see them just from the way they smell and feel." She ran her fingers over the delicate petals, and he immediately had a very ungentlemanly thought about how and where he'd like her fingers to be touching his anatomy. He grinned at the thought of how she would blush if he voiced the thought.

"The gardens are the jewel of the palace," he told her, touching her arm lightly so she could place where he was. He was learning the value of small actions such as this for her. "They were first designed and planted more than eleven thousand years ago, before Atlantis was forced to sink beneath the seas to escape invaders."

Lyric was the jewel of the garden. In a bright red sweater that wrapped around her in ways he shouldn't be thinking about and snug black pants, she shone like one of her own paintings against the backdrop of the flowers. He took a long, slow, steadying breath against the urge to pull her into his arms right there in the middle of the path.

"Is it a large garden? I'd love to walk through all of it." Her eyes closed in what looked like bliss as she walked slowly from flower to flower, touching them all.

"It's enormous. We will certainly walk through as much of it as you like, but perhaps first we should find you a place to stay."

She turned her head to face him. "I'm not—I'm not staying with you?"

Her voice came out small and hesitant, with perhaps a touch of hurt underlying her words. He hated himself for putting it there, for causing the shadow to cross her face, but the unfortunate truth was that he didn't have any quarters to take her to. When he was in port, he always stayed on his ship, and she wouldn't be comfortable there.

He fumbled about for a way to explain. "Well. About that—"

"Dare! I'm so glad you're safe." The voice was one he very rarely heard but recognized instantly. He suppressed a groan and the simultaneous instinct to flee, and turned to the newcomer.

He bowed. "Your Highness."

The queen of Atlantis didn't look especially royal at the moment. Her long, red-gold waves of hair were tied up and back from her face, and she wore a simple white shirt and blue jeans. Old, battered red running shoes completed the outfit. She looked more like one of the palace gardeners than a ruler. Better yet, she gave off the impression that she was much more comfortable like this than she'd been when he'd seen her in gowns and jewels at formal occasions. He liked her for it.

Next to him, Lyric stiffened, but then offered a nervous smile in Queen Riley's direction.

"I'm sorry. I have no idea how to curtsy," she blurted out.

The queen laughed, her bright blue eyes sparkling, and Dare liked her even better for that.

"Please. No 'Your Highness,' no bowing, no curtsying. It wasn't that long ago I was a social worker in Seattle. I certainly don't intend to put on fancy airs just because I happened to move to a new neighborhood."

Riley took Lyric's hands in hers and smiled at her, probably not realizing that Lyric couldn't see it.

"That's some zip code change," Lyric said wryly. "It's very nice to meet you. I'm Lyric Fielding."

Riley squeezed Lyric's hands and then released them and stepped back, her eyes widening. "You're not—but you must be. Lyric Fielding is an unusual name. I can't believe there are two of you. Lyric Fielding, the artist?"

Lyric smiled shyly, and then nodded. "I guess I am. I haven't heard of any other Lyric Fielding, so yeah, that's me."

Dare looked back and forth between them. "You know her work?"

"I do," Queen Riley said happily, leading Lyric with a gentle touch on the back of one elbow toward the fountain. "We can sit here if you have a moment."

The two women sat on the broad rim of the fountain, and the splashing of the water made a musical counterpoint to the sounds of their voices.

"I've loved your work for years," the queen was telling

Lyric. "I saw two small seascapes in an exhibition at the Seattle Museum of Art four years ago or so, and I've been following you ever since, hoping I could afford a painting one day. There's not much in the media about you, though."

Lyric bent her head so her face was turned toward her hands instead of toward Queen Riley. "Thank you. I—that's very nice of you. I've had requests for interviews and articles, but they weren't really things I wanted to follow up on. They ... they always seem to want to focus on the wrong thing, as far as I was concerned. And you don't have to buy a painting. Please allow me to offer you one as a gift."

Riley's mouth dropped open. "I wasn't—I didn't—oh, no. That's a lovely gesture, but I wasn't hinting for a gift. I'll tell my husband I've finally decided what I want for Christmas."

Lyric shook her head. "Please, allow me to—"

"No, really. You have no idea how happy he'll be. He tried watching American TV and decided I wanted a set of steak knives or life insurance. He has no idea what life insurance is, of course, but he said 'if such venerable old men are offering it, it must be of value.'"

Lyric laughed, but Dare had no idea why. King Conlan's reasoning was sound.

"Okay, then," Lyric said, still flashing her brilliant smile. "But only to save you from steak knives."

Riley laughed, but then grimaced. "Oh, and believe me, I completely understand about the interviews. The media requests I've gotten since Atlantis came back up from under the sea and decided to participate in world affairs have mostly been downright bizarre.. You would not believe the things people ask me."

The queen sat up straight, peered interestedly at Dare and Lyric, and began to speak in a weirdly falsetto voice. "Do you and the king have sex underwater? Does he have gills?"

Lyric burst out laughing and so did Dare, surprising even himself. It had been a long while since he heard himself laugh, at least while sober or in his right mind. He wasn't sure what he'd done last night in the grip of the fever, but it must've been interesting, considering the way Lyric's cheeks had turned pink this morning every time he'd even touched her hand.

"Dare, are Liam and his new wife here?" The queen turned toward him. "Jaime was incredibly helpful at Halloween. She planned the most amazing party, and everything was absolutely perfect."

Dare studied the queen's too-innocent face, wondering if he'd heard the faintest undertone of suggestion that Queen Riley actually knew all about the chaos and mishaps that had gone on behind the scenes on Halloween. Thieves had tried to steal the crown jewels and might've gotten away with it if his new sister-in-law hadn't been so quick-thinking. Liam probably had something to do with it too.

Mr. Perfect.

But Dare looked at Lyric, and the thought of the brother to whom he could never measure up didn't sting as much as it usually did. So Liam had perfection, and respect, and a new wife.

Dare had Lyric.

He realized Queen Riley was watching him expectantly. Oh, right. Jaime.

"I like her a lot," he admitted to the queen. "She's smart and funny and keeps Liam on his toes, which is certainly something he needs to knock a little bit of that arrogant pomposity out of him. She called him a fruit ninja."

Lyric laughed and then tilted her face up toward him. "I would've liked to have met him, but you said he was gone?"

"Yes, he and Jaime went to some village called Chicago to pack up her belongings and bring them back here."

Lyric and the queen started laughing, and he narrowed his eyes. "What did I say? Why is that funny?"

"Some village called Chicago," the queen said to Lyric, her eyes sparkling.

"I wonder what the Cubs fans would think about that," Lyric said, still laughing a little.

Riley stood and touched her on the shoulder.

"I'm delighted to meet you, Lyric. I'd love to talk some more, but I need to go see what my son is up to. Probably terrorizing his nanny. And no—I can't believe I have a nanny, either." She smiled ruefully. "It's another Cinderella moment. But anyway, I'd love to offer you rooms in the palace, if you're staying for a while. I have a beautiful place in mind, and you could use the adjacent room for a studio. There's a gorgeous balcony, and the light is magnificent—"

The queen abruptly stopped speaking, a horrified expression coming over her face. "I'm sorry. I imagine the light doesn't matter. Oh, wow, this is horribly awkward, so I'm just going to apologize for being a buffoon and leave it at that and hope you forgive me."

Lyric stood, too, and smiled in the queen's direction. "You have no idea how refreshing it is to have you acknowledge the awkwardness. People say stuff all the time, like 'Do you see what I mean?' and 'Will you look at that?' and then they get horribly awkward and weird, and it's ridiculous. They're figures of speech, and of course I know that. I've been blind since I was ten, and I'm not overly sensitive about things like that anymore."

Dare reached out almost without realizing it and took Lyric's hand. Her lips parted in surprise, but she squeezed his fingers in reassurance—whether for him or for herself, he couldn't tell.

Riley's large eyes considered Dare thoughtfully, and he suddenly and unpleasantly remembered that she was *aknasha'an*—an emotional empath. She could probably sense everything he was feeling, which meant he was five kinds of fool for not even trying to guard his emotions from her.

She smiled at him suddenly, eyes sparkling, and he wondered how the king and the high priest—former high priest—could stand to be involved with empaths. There'd never be any secrets.

The queen delicately cleared her throat. "The rooms?"

"That is very kind of you, Your Highness," Dare said. "I stay on my ship, of course, but I would much rather that Lyric had more comfortable accommodations."

"That would be lovely. Thank you so much," Lyric said, sounding as excited as a child. "I can't believe I'm going to stay in the *palace*."

"I still haven't gotten used to it," the queen admitted. "Perfect. I'll have someone show you to the rooms I have in mind and make sure they're set up for company and for you to paint, if you like. If you wouldn't mind, I'd love to stop by and talk to you about your painting sometime. If that's okay."

Lyric's smile was like a burst of sunshine spreading across her face. It was as if she were glowing—actually *glowing*—with happiness. Even the curls on her head suddenly looked bouncier. A hard, cold knot that had crouched inside Dare's chest for a very long time cracked open just a little, and he swallowed hard.

"Thank you so much, Your, um—"

"Riley," the queen said firmly. "Just Riley, please."

"Thank you so much, Riley," Lyric said. "I happily accept, and I would love for you to come by and talk to me about painting. I promise not to ask anything about gills or underwater sex, kings or otherwise."

Riley laughed. "We can talk about villages. Like Chicago."

She darted a glance at Dare, who was still bewildered by why a village named Chicago was funny, but he enjoyed watching Lyric smile too much to complain about it.

With a quick goodbye, the queen was gone, heading toward the palace and the little prince.

Lyric leaned over and trailed her fingers in the water for a few moments and then turned toward him. "I realize that I never asked you about brothers and sisters. It seems strange, considering we've known each other for so long—but on the other hand, we haven't known each other long at all. It hasn't really been six years, just maybe a total of thirty or so days during the six years that we saw each other." Lyric shoved her waves of chestnut curls out of her face after a tendril of breeze brushed by. The sun burnished her hair with glints of gold and copper, and suddenly he yearned to run his fingers through her curls. He took a step toward her, not even a little sure of what he was going to do next, but then she spoke again.

"Is it only Liam? Liam and you?"

"Actually, no. We have another brother. Flynn. But we haven't seen him in a few years. The last I heard, he was caught up with a bad gang of dragon shifters. Real lowlifes."

Her eyebrows drew together. "There are dragon shifters? Wow. I had no idea."

He put her hand on his arm, picked up the bags, and started walking with her toward the palace. By now, the queen would have someone ready to show them to Lyric's rooms.

"Yes, there are dragon shifters," he said. "There are all sorts of different shifters. I once heard about a koala shifter who kept falling asleep on the job until he finally switched to the night shift. And I'm actually friends with— or at least acquaintances with—a pretty badass tiger shifter who lives down in your neck of the woods."

She walked beside him, unhesitant but cautious about where she placed her steps. He slowed, cursing himself for a fool because he'd started out at his normal, long-striding pace. She didn't know this place like she knew her own neighborhood back in St. Augustine. He had to be more careful with her.

She wasn't fragile; he knew that. But she was precious to him and, like all precious things, must be treated with care.

A nasty voice in his mind reminded him that fragile things didn't fare very well in the hands of pirates. He blocked the voice and its message firmly into a steel compartment in the back of his brain, labeled 'things to think about later.'"

"I'm so glad your ship and crew are safe," she said, changing the subject. "If you want to go check on them once we find my room, of course you should. I *am* fine on my own, you know."

"I know you are. You run your own business. You have your own studio. You are in complete control of your own life, and I admire the hell out of you for it." He put every bit of sincerity he felt into his voice, since she couldn't see it in his face. "But I *would* like to go see my ship and talk to my crew, so if—"

Dare. I have more news.

The guard's voice in his mind sounded hesitant, and Dare lost patience with that quickly.

What is it? Tell me now, man.

It's your ship. It's... it's no longer your ship. Poseidon has decreed that you're not to step even one foot on board.

He froze and then reached again for the armband that was no longer on his arm.

"Apparently my ship is no longer my ship," he told Lyric carefully, trying not to let his anger leak into his voice. "I need to find out what's going on, and I really, really need to find out about Seranth. I haven't been able to sense her since I came through the portal into your house without my armband."

Lyric touched his cheek. "I'm sure she's okay. She is a sea spirit, after all. You said she's existed for thousands of years. I doubt a little storm—or even a huge storm—could harm her. But please go find out."

They reached one of the many doors to the palace, where one of the people who worked there stood smiling at Lyric. "Welcome to Atlantis, Ms. Fielding. I'm Fergus, and Queen Riley has asked me to show you to your rooms. If you'll come this way?"

"May I place my hand on your arm?" Lyric asked calmly, with no hesitation, and Fergus, in return, didn't blink or hesitate.

"Of course." He stepped closer and held out his arm. "Just at your left," he told her.

"Go," Lyric urged Dare. "I'm almost as anxious as you are to hear. Find me when you get back."

"I will. I'll be back soon."

"Take your time, I look forward to walking through my first real palace. I feel like a princess already," Lyric said, smiling at both men.

Fergus looked as bowled over by the force of the smile as Dare felt. And Fergus was seventy years old if he was a day. That smile of hers charmed everyone.

She hesitated, and then put her hand out, fingers splayed like the most slender and delicate of starfish, until she touched his chest. Then she stood on her tiptoes and kissed Dare's cheek. "I'll see you soon, I hope."

Oh, no. Cheek kisses were not happening. He placed the bags on the ground, wrapped one arm around her, and kissed her. A single, quick, but very deliberate kiss. "Count on it."

She blinked and then drew a shaky breath, looking a little dazed, and he felt a smug smile quirking at the edges of his lips. He might not deserve her love, but he'd be damned if he'd settle for only her friendship.

Fergus, who'd been very carefully looking anywhere but at them, then took Lyric's arm. "Shall we go, my lady?"

"Lyric, please," she said, still sounding bemused.

Dare smiled and watched her walk off with Fergus. He'd just go find out about Seranth and what in the *hells* was up with his ship—

Suddenly Poseidon's voice smashed into Dare's mind with the force of a massive hammer, laying waste to his too-recently healed head.

DO NOT WASTE YOUR TIME COMING TO FIND SERANTH. I HAVE DISSOLVED YOUR BOND, AND NOW SHE IS FREE TO FIND A CAPTAIN WHO ISN'T A SELFISH ASS.

When his head stopped ringing, Dare realized he'd fallen to his knees, almost knocked unconscious by the sea god's wrath. He stood up, brushed off his pants, and nodded once, sharply. "You can stick your Trident up your ass. The pointy end. I'm getting Seranth *and* my ship back, whether you like it or not."

The sea god roared at him, but Dare didn't give a damn. He'd defied worse odds.

But when he started walking, and then running, toward the docks and his ship, a little voice in his mind laughed at him. He snarled at it.

A little denial never hurt anybody.

S *o now Della's beautiful hair fell about her rippling and* *shining like a cascade of brown waters. It reached below* *her knee and made itself almost a garment for her. And* *then she did it up again nervously and quickly. Once she faltered* *for a minute and stood still while a tear or two splashed on the* *worn red carpet.*

On went her old brown jacket; on went her old brown hat. *With a whirl of skirts and with the brilliant sparkle still in her* *eyes, she fluttered out the door and down the stairs to the street.*

Where she stopped the sign read: "Mne. Sofronie. Hair Goods *of All Kinds." One flight up Della ran, and collected herself, pant-* *ing. Madame, large, too white, chilly, hardly looked the* *"Sofronie."*

"Will you buy my hair?" asked Della.

-- The Gift of the Magi, O. Henry (1917)

S he was in Atlantis.

She was in *Atlantis.*

Lyric kept wanting to pinch herself or giggle like a little

girl. She'd spent the past year practicing all the ways she could invite Dare to stay in St. Augustine with her for Christmas, and he'd scooped her completely by inviting her to Atlantis. And here she was.

In Atlantis.

She laughed with the sheer joy of it and felt Fergus pause next to her. He made an inquisitive noise, and she smiled.

"It's like a dream, isn't it? I mean, I know you've probably lived here all your life, but to us—to me—Atlantis was a myth or a legend. The lost city. Almost certainly fictional. And now, to be here, to actually be here in person is just amazing." She felt like she was babbling, but she didn't mind that much. She figured it was a pretty normal human reaction to stepping into the center of a fairytale.

"Yes, ma'am. Although I admit I feel a little bit that way about your place." He had a rich, kind-sounding voice, and she could hear the sincerity in it.

"Florida?" She thought about it. "I mean, St. Augustine is the most beautiful city in the U.S., if I do say so myself, but I doubt it can compare to Atlantis. Plus, you have water on all sides. We only have it on the one."

He laughed. "No, ma'am, not Florida. Earth. Topside. Most of us have never been anywhere but Atlantis our entire lives."

She mentally smacked her forehead. Of course. Atlantis had been protected by a magical dome far beneath the ocean for a little more than eleven thousand years, before some super-magical high priest had managed to make the city rise to the surface.

She'd listen to a special about it on *60 Minutes*. And she'd heard that *People* magazine had put cover photos of the king and queen on almost every issue for months after

Atlantis appeared. There had been a huge hubbub of excitement all over social media, Meredith told her, about the king of Atlantis choosing an American bride.

"Well, you're invited to visit me anytime," she told Fergus, "And please call me Lyric. Ma'am makes me feel old."

It didn't, really. And he hadn't asked a single thing about her blindness, which was unusual and refreshing in a new acquaintance. She could feel the tense muscles in her neck and shoulders begin to relax, and she took a long, deep breath and then slowly exhaled.

Releasing stress for the universe to take care of, as Meredith would say. Thinking of Meredith made her realize how much her friend would love this place. If only Meredith were here, she could describe what everything looked like. Lyric didn't quite feel comfortable enough to ask Dare to serve as Seeing Eye person just yet, and certainly not Fergus. She sighed, but then forced the momentary trickle of discomfort away.

She was in Atlantis. No negativity of any sort today.

They turned a corner and Fergus took a few steps and then stopped. "Would you like for me to describe what our surroundings as we walk, Miss? A tour, so to speak?"

Happiness sang through her. A personal tour of Atlantis with a guide who knew it well. "That would be lovely. Thank you."

He cleared his throat. "Ah...will it be relevant to describe colors?"

It was a very sensitive and perceptive question. She knew colors since she hadn't been blind since birth, but of course he'd had no way of knowing that. She found herself blinking rapidly as a flood of warmth swept through her, but she smiled her biggest smile. "Thank you. Yes, please."

"This is the throne room," Fergus said beside her. He cleared his throat. "The room is flanked with white marble columns, in which veins of an Atlantean metal called orichalcum—almost exactly the color of your eyes, Miss—are inset into designs of dolphins leaping and a bunch of Nereids laughing at their mermaid play."

"Nereids? I don't know that, but it sounds Greek and vaguely familiar," she said, racking her brain for the reference but coming up empty.

"The Nereids were sea nymphs and friends of Poseidon, beautiful and kind. They often helped humans," he told her.

Light dawned. "Oh, right. I know them now. They helped Jason and the Argonauts, right?"

Fergus made a tsking sound. "The Argonauts. Humph."

She waited, but he seemed disinclined to say anything further, so she switched topics. "And that amazing scent? What flower is that?" She inhaled deeply, wanting to walk across the entire continent, simply smelling everything.

"Ah. That's the lava-tulips. They're green and blue, and they smell like ambrosia," Fergus told her. "They're my favorites. And then the throne is set up high on that dais—"

"It sounds amazing and a little intimidating," she said, and then she paused, hearing voices and laughter just before she heard the footsteps coming toward her.

"That's why we never hang out here," said a deep male voice. "It makes me itch."

Lyric heard female laughter from the person standing next to the man who'd spoken.

"Ven, cut it out. You'll make our guest feel like we're all barbarians."

Lyric turned toward them and smiled. "What? I was promised barbarians. Where are the barbarians?"

"Hello. I'm Erin. I'm married to the barbarian," the woman said fondly.

"I'm Ven, and I can tell I'm gonna like you a lot," Ven said, laughter in his voice.

"Fergus, we're going to steal this lovely lady and take her to lunch, if that's all right with her," Erin said. "If that's okay with you, Lyric?"

Lyric didn't hesitate for a single second. "That sounds awesome. I admit I hadn't thought of food in all the excitement, but now that you brought it up, I realize I'm starving. I'm Lyric Fielding—wait. You just called me Lyric. So I guess you know who I am."

Maybe Atlantis was more like home than she could have imagined. Gossip traveled here at the speed of light, too.

"I'll just take your bags to your room, Miss Fielding," Fergus said. "Queen Riley has put her in the top floor suite in the east wing, Princess."

"Princess?" Lyric suddenly felt like a fish out of water; no Atlantean pun intended. Or that she was waking up in a Disney movie. There was royalty everywhere she turned. If somebody asked her to kiss a frog, she was out of there.

"Just Erin, Fergus. Please, don't make me turn you into a toad." There was the sound of real affection in Erin's voice, and Fergus chuckled.

"Right. Erin. And I learned long ago not to call Lord Vengeance 'Your Highness,' or, as he repeatedly proclaimed, he'd kick my ass."

"Lord Vengeance?" Lyric was getting confused.

"Ven is technically the Lord Vengeance to his brother the king," Erin said. "Not just a big lovable goofball."

Of course he was. Now she had a queen, a princess, and a prince who was also a lord. It would have been a great poker hand. For a painter who'd been raised by a tour bus guide, it was heady stuff.

Fergus, still at Lyric's side, cleared his throat. "The *lovable goofball* is one of Atlantis's fiercest warriors, as you well know, Princess."

"If only everyone else were as smart as you, Fergus," Ven said ruefully.

"Thank you, Fergus," Lyric said. "Would you like to join us for lunch, too?"

"Why, that's very nice of you to ask. But I have a busy afternoon in front of me, and a lunch date with a beautiful girl I'll be late for if I don't hurry," Fergus told her, patting her arm.

"How is that granddaughter of yours, Fergus?" Ven laughed. "You can tell she definitely gets her looks from her grandmother."

"Ah, yes. Princely humor," Fergus said with amusement. "Did I mention how lucky we all are that you were born second?"

Lyric gasped, but nobody heard her in the burst of laughter that followed, and she realized they must all have been joking with each other. This didn't sound at all like any kind of royal/servant relationship she'd ever read about.

She had to admit, she really liked it.

Her stomach picked that embarrassing moment to growl quite loudly, and she clapped her hand over it and felt herself blushing. "Oh my gosh. I'm really sorry."

"My stomach feels the same way," Ven told her. "May I take your arm?"

She nodded, and he gently took her hand and put it on his arm. "Food, Erin. Onward."

They ate at a table on a small terrace that Ven told her overlooked the garden, but she could have guessed that from the gentle breeze that lifted her hair off her neck and carried the delicate aroma of Atlantean flowers.

Oh, and the *food*. It was one of the most delicious lunches Lyric could ever remember eating. The main course was a spicy white fish wrapped in pastry, and there were so many vegetables and fruits to choose from that she was too full to eat another bite long before the dishes stopped coming. She drank a glass of a light, fruity wine

"All of this is from our own gardens, and of course we have a fleet of people very happy to be able to fish again," Ven said.

"Sounds amazing," she said honestly. "I feel like I could happily be a gardener in Atlantis for a while. It must be like a dream to live here and tend these plants. And the colors. Oh. The colors must be miraculous."

She took another sip of wine and then laughed. "Of course, I could be totally wrong. Atlantean flowers could all be uniformly gray."

"Nope. We have all the colors you have in your flowers, and a few more, I think. You'd have to talk to people who know more about it than me, but I can arrange something if you'd like," Ven said.

Before Lyric could reply, Erin, who'd become increasingly quiet during lunch, cleared her throat. "So. Lyric. When did you first realize you're a gem singer?"

Lyric dropped her spoon out of suddenly nerveless fingers. "A—a what?"

"My wife is a witch, yes, but she's also a gem singer," Ven said gently. "A person whose soul's magic resonates with the spirit of the stones of the Earth. Some records indicate it was primarily a talent of the elvenfolk among the Fae, but it was well known in ancient Atlantis."

He laughed. "Hey, and welcome to the family. The last

recording of a gem singer in Fae history was before the Cataclysm that sank Atlantis. You also may be part Atlantean."

Lyric drew in a shaky breath but said nothing. Her voice didn't seem to be working anymore. She might be *Atlantean?* She'd known something was up with the magic and the stones, of course she'd known, although she'd tried not to think too hard about exactly what. But Atlantean?

This was a down-the-rabbit-hole moment, if she'd ever had one. A shiver that had nothing to do with being cold snaked down her spine, but then she dazedly realized Erin was telling her something.

"...and clearly your magic—your art—resonates with gems. My magic is also greatly magnified through their use. So I recognized you, of course. Like calls to like. When did you first realize?" Erin's voice was kind but also implacable, as if she meant to find out everything, even and maybe especially Lyric's secrets to which she had no right, fellow 'gem singer' or not.

But witch or not, princess or not, Erin had never tangled with Lyric Fielding before.

"I'm not sure what you mean," Lyric said brightly. "I never sing, except in church. Speaking of which, I hear you're planning your first Christmas here this year. I have a stellar recipe for a mean gingerbread cookie, if you're interested."

Erin blew out a breath. "Okay. I get it. None of my business. But if you ever want to talk about it, I'm here."

The kindness in her voice made Lyric feel a little guilty, but not guilty enough to share the most private secret in her life. Maybe sometime she could open up to the princess—and she'd surely love to have some answers--but not just yet.

An icy wind swept across the table, and she shivered.

"It's suddenly quite cold, isn't it? I should have brought a sweater."

"No need. That's just Alaric," Ven said. "Hey, bro. How's it hanging?"

A deep voice that sounded like an avalanche spoke next. "I'll ignore you as usual, Ven. Why is there a gem-singing artist at your table?"

"Lunch," Erin said sweetly. "Perhaps you've heard of it. It's a meal civilized people eat between breakfast and dinner. Even former high priests must eat lunch."

"Sometimes there's second breakfast," Ven pointed out.

"Only if you're a hobbit," Lyric added, and then couldn't believe she'd spoken up with the scary, demanding guy looming over her, blocking what little bit of the sun she could sense.

Alaric bent down closer to her—she could tell because the cold sensation of magic he'd brought with him intensified, sharpening almost to the point of pain—and took her chin in his hand, moving her head around as if she were an interesting specimen.

Of course, to him she might be.

She swallowed hard, but then yanked her face out of his grasp. "I beg your pardon."

"Most do," he said dryly. "It never helps them, though. Have you tried magic— either from the witches or from a healer—to heal your eyes?"

Lyric clenched her hands into fists in her lap so as not to punch him in the face. That probably *would* cause an international incident. Or her impending demise. But she was a little tired and a lot overwhelmed, and she wished Dare would show up. She was too much of an introvert to really enjoy extended periods of time with large groups of people she didn't know. And this— this was a very personal question.

Apparently, however, there were no barriers to what Atlanteans felt they could ask one lone human woman.

She put a little steel in her voice and answered him. "Please step back. You are invading my personal space. Yes. I've consulted with witches and other types of magical healers. It's not possible for my eyes to be saved. There was too much damage."

"Alaric might be able to help you," Erin said quietly. "He has more magic than anyone I've ever known or heard about."

"I *am* magic," Alaric said flatly. It wasn't even arrogance; that's what was so terrifying. It was a simple statement of fact to him, she was sure.

"Hate to admit it, but he's telling the truth," Ven put in. "He has more magic than any high priest in the history of Atlantis, which is to say more magic than anyone in the history of the world. If he says he can fix you, he can."

And there it was.

It took Lyric a long time to hit tilt, but when she did, it was an explosive blast. And right now she was pulling out the matches and lighting the TNT.

She gripped the wooden arms of her chair so tightly she wouldn't have been surprised to hear them crack. "I beg your pardon, *Your Highness.* Mr. Magic. I do not need to be *fixed.* Blindness is not a *defect.* It's simply another state of being. Kind of like the state of being where you exist in a higher plane of arrogant assholishness and presume to know whom you should go around *fixing.*"

There was a long silence, and then Ven whistled. "She's got us there, man. I think she just handed me my head."

"And you deserved it," his wife said coldly. "I think all of us have tried to strong-arm our guest enough today. She probably hates us, and we'd deserve it. Damn. I'm just as bad as they are. I'm sorry, Lyric."

"Nobody thinks you're defective, Lyric," Ven said quietly. "We may be big, strong warriors, but we bumble around like orangutans on caffeine sometimes. But we meant well, so please don't take offense."

Lyric blew out a long breath, sudden exhaustion overcoming her anger. There was suddenly just too much—too much sensation, too much new sensory input, too much unfamiliarity and presumption. It all combined to drop on her shoulders and mind with a heavy weight. "I'm sorry. I'm so sorry. I'm a guest here, and that was unspeakably rude of me. Thank you for your concern, Ven, Erin. Alaric. I'm sorry to be prickly about it. I just get awfully tired of that particular point of view."

She heard the sound of the chair next to her sliding out and that side of her body cooled. Alaric, then. He must be sitting next to her. "May I touch you?"

She was startled by the grave courtesy in his voice, especially after "assholishness," which was a new low, even for her. Damn. She'd probably end up on *60 Minutes* next, as the American who'd ruined diplomatic relations between the U.S. and Atlantis.

"Miss Fielding?"

Alaric's voice startled her out of her mental ramblings. In spite of very serious reservations, she felt like she had to agree. Apology, international relations, any hope of a future with Dare...she didn't know which reason to pick, but the combined weight of them forced her to say yes.

"Yes. But don't do anything to me without my knowledge and explicit consent," she warned him.

His touch, when it came, was on her forehead, feather-light, and only lasted a few seconds.

"I am truly sorry, Miss Fielding," Alaric said. "The damage is too extensive. There is nothing I can do."

Even though she'd expected nothing—even though she wasn't sure she'd accept 'fixing' if offered—the bleak words were like a punch in the stomach, and she literally doubled over in pain.

Erin's lighter touch settled on her shoulder. "Lyric! Are you all right?"

Lyric managed to get her breath under control and nodded. "It's just...it's just the loss of the possibility. I don't—"

A horrible thought occurred to her. "You didn't...Alaric. You didn't say that because I was so rude to you, did you?"

"The rudeness was my own," Alaric said softly. "I apologize for it, but it had nothing to do with my conclusion. The trauma is not something I can heal. I will contact you immediately should I ever discover a way to change that, if you would be agreeable."

"I—yes. Thank you. I really...would it be possible for someone to take me to my room? I'm quite tired," she said, clenching her jaw to keep from breaking down.

"*There* you are," Dare's voice called from across the terrace, his footsteps rapidly approaching.

She blew out a breath, her entire body relaxing at the thought that *here* he was: haven. Sanctuary.

Dare.

He strode across the terrace directly toward her, and she pushed back her chair and stood. Afraid to try to walk toward him, because she was unsure of what obstacles were in her way. Afraid to stay where she was, in case she had an emotional breakdown of some sort.

Relieved beyond measure when his footsteps, coming closer, sped up.

"I found you—" he began, but then his voice hardened. "What is the matter? What happened?"

"I...nothing. I'm just—"

He reached her and pulled her into his arms, and she'd never been so glad to be anywhere.

"What did you do to her?" he demanded, and she heard chairs pushing back from the table. "I don't care if you're high priest or not, if you harmed a single hair on her head, you *will* answer for it."

Lyric's breath caught in her throat. This voice—this side of Dare--was one she didn't know. This was the voice of a predator; the sound of implacable darkness that would stalk the night and make all lesser beings run.

And she'd caused it by being stupid and weak.

A hideous flare of embarrassment washed through her. "No! No, they were so nice, it just...I just...I'm just tired. Please, can we go to my room?"

She could feel Dare's body tense, as if he were straining toward the others, but then he pushed out a long, controlled breath.

"Lyric, are you sure you want to spend time with the pirate?" Ven asked abruptly, all traces of humor in his voice gone. "We can make sure--"

"Try and take her," Dare growled.

"There was no injury, Dare," Erin said calmly. "I think we can all calm down now, please. Don't make me send you to your rooms, boys."

There was a silence, and then Ven laughed. "You do realize that's not a punishment, since you live in my rooms, too, honey?"

The tension in the air dropped by several degrees, and

Lyric took a deep breath. "What Erin said. Calm down or I'll start singing Christmas carols. Loudly. Off-key."

"Ooh, yes. Jingle Bells," Erin said

"I have no patience for this," Alaric said, and then another icy breeze swept by Lyric.

"Is he gone? Just poof?" she said, stepping back from where she'd been standing clutching Dare. "My singing isn't that bad."

"Mine is," Erin said cheerfully, and then she started to sing. "Jingle Bells, Jingle Bells…"

Lyric joined in and they sang the entire song. "…oh, what fun it is to ride in a one horse open sleigh."

By the time they were done, it seemed like Dare and Ven were cordial again, but Lyric was worn out and needed some time away from strangers.

"Thank you so much for lunch. But if you don't mind, I'm a little tired now," she said.

Erin stepped closer and touched Lyric's arm. "We're here if you need us."

When they'd gone, Dare moved closer to her again. "I have something…Well." He cleared his throat. "I thought this might…Here. Just hold this for me for luck. I brought it from my private collection just for you."

He took her hand and placed something in her palm, and then folded her fingers around it. It was about the size of a quail egg, and felt cool at first, but then heated up quickly.

"What—"

"It's an amethyst. I thought it would be good…it would help you paint. Or something," he said, his voice trailing off, and suddenly—if she hadn't known better—she would have thought he sounded shy. "I want you to have it."

"Oh, Dare, I can't take this…Wait." She inhaled sharply

as the stone heated up even more quickly, to the point where it was nearly, but not quite, burning her hand, and then it started to sing. "What's happening?"

Dare answered something, but she didn't hear the words. Sounds, all sounds, faded into a dreamy background of white noise as the gem's tones pulled her into its magic, and begged her to sing to it.

"Lyric? Lyric!"

Someone was holding her arms and shaking her, but it didn't matter. *He* didn't matter. Only the magic. She was *holding* the magic, and it wanted to hear her song. She smiled and twirled around, laughing and crying, and then took a deep breath and began to sing a song she'd never heard before, and the world burst into brilliant, blinding light around her.

She sang, and cried, and laughed, and she clutched the amethyst to her chest, dancing on the terrace, on the lawn, on air. It was as if she'd opened a door and walked directly into an Impressionist painting by one of the masters; as if she danced inside the paint on the canvases at the *Musée d'Orsay* in Paris she'd visited with her parents when she was a child.

She laughed out loud, delighting in the shapes and the colors and the light—oh, the lovely, *spectacular* light—and then he was there. Holding her in his arms.

Keeping her safe.

"I know you," she told him, smiling with utter and complete joy. "You are important to me."

The light tried to take her again, and the stone demanded her song, so she tried to pull away from him, no matter that he was important, no matter that she...*loved him?*

Yes. She knew this. She loved him. He was her love.

The amethyst pulsed again, against her heart, and she

suddenly *saw him.* She saw through the starburst of color and light—*so much light*—to his dark silhouette directly in front of her. She reached out to touch his face, but unknowingly, she'd reached out with the hand holding the gem, and the moment the back of her fingers touched his skin, a jolt like a lightning strike ran through her, and she could see his face.

She could see his face.

The shapes and angles of it—the colors. His hair was so black as to be almost blue, and his eyes were the deep, drowning blue of the ocean seen from St. Augustine Beach in the middle of summer.

He was beautiful—he was *beautiful.* Entirely masculine, from the planes and angles of his face to his sensual lips to his straight, Roman nose. Even the dark lashes that surrounded his unbelievable glowing eyes contributed to his beauty.

Her knees gave out, literally gave out, like a swooning maiden's in a children's tale.

She didn't care.

"I can see you, Dare. I can *see* you."

She was laughing, but she didn't know she was crying until she felt the tears running down her face.

"I can see you," she repeated. "And you're *beautiful.*"

"I buy hair," said Madame. "Take yer hat off and let's have a sight at the looks of it."

Down rippled the brown cascade.

"Twenty dollars," said Madame, lifting the mass with a practiced hand.

"Give it to me quick," said Della.

Oh, and the next two hours tripped by on rosy wings. Forget the hashed metaphor. She was ransacking the stores for Jim's present.

-- The Gift of the Magi, O. Henry (1917)

"You're so beautiful," she said again, this time whispering as if only to herself. "Your eyes glow. They're glowing, Dare. All that lovely dark blue, but with a hint of green in the centers. How can I see this? How can I see this?"

He put his hands on her hips to steady her because it seemed as if she might float away into the air. As if gravity itself had lost its hold on her.

"This has never happened to you before?" He said it tentatively, but he wanted to know. He *needed* to know.

She shook her head, clutching the jewel, and brushed the tears away with the back of one hand.

"Never. I have a... talent. A gift, I call it. This is going to sound ridiculous, or at least very strange—"

He snatched an unused cloth napkin from the table and gently wiped her face. "I just brought you to Atlantis. How can anything you say to me be more ridiculous than that?"

His lame attempt at a joke accomplished its end; she smiled and even laughed a little.

"Okay. Here it is: when I sing to the gemstones, I can sometimes see a little bit. I know it sounds crazy, but it's true. Erin just called me a gem singer. They said I might be part Atlantean! It's true that when I use the jewels in my paints, I can see the play of light and darkness in the paints and in the images I create."

Her copper-colored eyes were large and shining. In fact, her entire face seemed lit from within.

"I'm kind of surprised you don't walk around carrying gemstones all the time then," he said, puzzled.

"You don't think I've tried? It doesn't work that way. The jewel magic—that's what I call it—it only works with my art. When I'm creating art. It has only ever worked when I'm painting, no matter the gemstone. I even tried more rare and valuable gemstones in case that made a difference. But a piece of quartz works just as well as a diamond."

"Then why now—"

"I don't know," she cried. "I don't know, but I don't want to lose this feeling. The paintings I could create with this..."

He took her hand and squeezed it. "Let's walk in the gardens while we talk about this."

She beamed up at him. "That's a wonderful idea. I want to see what they look like now."

He tucked her hand into the crook of his elbow, and they left the terrace and started toward the middle of the gardens. Blazing color—a riot of beauty—lay spread out before them, and he could tell from her reaction that she was actually *seeing* it. Lyric's grip on his hand grew tighter and tighter until he wondered if she might break the bones in his fingers, but he couldn't bring himself to care because she was touching him. *Finally* touching him.

And singing.

She stopped, in the middle of the path about fifteen feet away from the fountain, her lips parted, eyes glowing, and her entire face incandescent with joy. He wanted to hold her and bask in her delight, to watch her forever.

Forever.

"I can hear the water, of course, but I can also ... see something. Oh, Dare, I can see—I can see the light flowing and cascading."

She whirled around and put both her hands on his chest, still gripping the amethyst. "Do you understand what that means? It means I'm actually *seeing* the water. I'm seeing the water play in the light in the fountain."

He pulled her closer—he couldn't help it. He wanted to kiss her, and hold her, and breathe in some of the brilliant light and joy surrounding her and shining from within her. But before he could bend his head to do so, she whirled around again, releasing him, and took a tentative step toward the fountain, then another and another until she was almost running. He dashed after her to make sure she didn't collide with the fountain's marble edge, but she stopped inches away.

Laughing.

Crying.

Emotions were pouring out of her faster than the water poured from the fountain, and she was still singing. The song sounded familiar, and he suddenly realized why. She was singing an ancient Temple song of gratitude for a full harvest...*in an ancient Atlantean dialect.*

How was that even possible? Had he somehow broken her mind by bringing her here?

"It's so much. It's too much. I don't know how to process all this." She turned to him, clutching her head with both hands. "It's overwhelming me, Dare. I need a moment. I think I... I need a moment in a quiet place to comprehend all of this."

"Are you sure?" He brushed a curl from her cheek and tucked it behind her ear. "What if...what if you can't ... what if this doesn't happen again?"

She shook her head and flung her arms out to the sides. "Of course I'm not sure. I'm terrified that if I walk out of this garden, this experience will never happen to me again. My head feels like it's about to split open, the way it used to feel right after the accident. Which makes me realize that I'm going to need to get some rest in a quiet place soon, or I might fall down and be out with a three-day migraine."

He studied her face and noted her narrowed eyes and clenched jaw, signs of strain that hadn't been there only a few moments before. "What's a migraine?"

"It's the worst headache that has ever existed. And—oh, no—it's starting now." She stumbled a little, reluctantly handing him the gem. He pocketed it quickly and then he swept her off the ground and into his arms, lifting her with one arm under her back and the other under her knees.

"I can walk, Dare," she hissed, "Put me down."

Her cheeks blushed a delightful pink, and he suddenly,

fiercely wanted to lay her down in the middle of all the flowers and take her. Hard and urgent. Claim her.

Possess her.

He had to clench his jaw shut to keep from kissing her, because kissing would lead to more, and he wasn't entirely sure that she would want him to stop. But he knew he was no good for her—could never be good for her.

There was no way in the nine hells he would allow his darkness to infect her light.

"I know you can walk, Lyric," he murmured into the shining cloud of her hair. "But this way I get the chance to play the hero, which will shock the hell out of people around here. Let me have a little fun, okay?"

She laughed a little but then winced, still holding her head. "Okay," she whispered.

He didn't wait. He headed for the palace with the steadiest and smoothest stride he could manage to avoid jolting her or causing her further pain. When they reached the palace, the cool shade seemed to help her. The furrows in her forehead smoothed out, and he felt her relax a little in his arms.

"I'm sorry, " she told him. "I don't know where my room is. Fergus took my things while we went to lunch."

"Don't worry. I know exactly the room Riley was talking about."

He walked up three double flights of stairs with her held tightly in his arms, grimly enjoying the shocked expressions on the faces of everyone he passed. He knew what they were thinking about him. Dare the pirate. Dare the reprobate.

Dare the scoundrel.

They probably thought he was taking this poor woman hostage to have his wicked way with her.

At the thought of wicked ways and Lyric both in the same sentence, his skin heated and his body hardened.

"Bad timing," he muttered.

"I'm sorry. I—"

"Not you, sweetheart. This was all on me."

When they arrived at the rooms Riley had given Lyric, he saw that Fergus had placed her bags neatly next to the bed, unopened. Atlanteans were very careful to preserve privacy for others, since close quarters under the dome had made retaining privacy essential to civilization. No one would've thought or dreamed of opening her bags.

Knowing Lyric, she probably would prefer it that way. Personally, he was wishing a night dress had been put out. He walked over and gently lowered Lyric to the bed.

"What can I do?" He studied her face, aching at the strained paleness of her beautiful features that had held such joy and light only minutes earlier. "Tell me. Anything."

"You've done enough already," she protested. "I just need to rest."

"I'll go get a healer or a glass of water. No, a glass of water *and* a healer. I'll get – I'll get the queen. I'll find some-body," he said, shocked at the torrent of words gushing out of his mouth.

How everyone would laugh to find the man they knew as coldhearted and steady in any crisis was terrified, but he *was* afraid. Afraid this headache—this migraine Lyric suffered might be the precursor to something worse. That whatever reaction had happened with the gemstones might have been the catalyst.

By the gods, if his gift had harmed her—if he were the reason for her pain—he would not want to live. He couldn't lose her. He couldn't. He'd already lost his ship and Seranth, but this loss …the truth of it sliced through him. This loss would break him.

She held out her hand, and he immediately took it in his own.

"Just stay with me. I don't need anything but sleep right now, but please stay with me," she asked softly.

"Always," he promised.

She smiled a little, but it wasn't until after he'd eased himself down on the bed next to her in a sitting position, and she'd moved to rest her head in his lap and fallen asleep, that he realized what he'd said.

How could he give *always* to a woman when he didn't even deserve her *now*?

8

She found it at last. It surely had been made for Jim and no one else. There was no other like it in any of the stores, and she had turned all of them inside out. It was a platinum fob chain simple and chaste in design, properly proclaiming its value by substance alone and not by meretricious ornamentation—as all good things should do. It was even worthy of The Watch. As soon as she saw it she knew that it must be Jim's. It was like him. Quietness and value—the description applied to both. Twenty-one dollars they took from her for it, and she hurried home with the 87 cents. With that chain on his watch Jim might be properly anxious about the time in any company. Grand as the watch was, he sometimes looked at it on the sly on account of the old leather strap that he used in place of a chain.

When Della reached home her intoxication gave way a little to prudence and reason. She got out her curling irons and lighted the gas and went to work repairing the ravages made by generosity added to love. Which is always a tremendous task, Dear friends--a mammoth task.

-- *The Gift of the Magi*, O. Henry (1917)

*S*he slept all afternoon. She slept through dinner; she slept through sunset. And throughout that time, all those many hours, he sat and held her, stroking the silk of her hair. Thanking the gods—both his and hers—for this brief moment of happiness in a long life that had been so seriously lacking in it. He nodded off a few times, for a few minutes at a time, but woke at her slightest motion or murmur. He would keep her safe, even from the enemy of her own mind, if need be.

Lyric began to wake at midnight. The dawn of a new day. It seemed fitting, somehow. She stretched, long and luxuriant, and he felt his body hardening in response. He was finally in bed with her, something he'd dreamed of—fantasized about—on many long, cold nights walking the deck of the ship.

But this wasn't exactly how he'd pictured it. First he had been injured, and now she was. It was all a great cosmic joke by someone with a very bad sense of humor.

She leaned her head back until it touched his abdomen. She froze, as if only then realizing that she'd been asleep curled up next to him with her head in his lap.

"Dare?"

"I certainly hope I'm the only man in your bed." He tried to make it sound like a joke, but it fell woefully flat. He knew he could have no claim to her future; she deserved better than a pirate. He couldn't even hope for a miracle, because he'd resolved to stop giving himself hope that he didn't deserve.

"I'm a pirate," he said, low and anguished. The words felt like they'd been ripped out of him, but he needed her to understand. He needed her to cast him aside, because he was becoming less and less sure he had the strength to leave her on his own.

She rolled onto her side and looked up at him. Although he supposed *looked* was the wrong word. Unless she could still see—but no. He'd taken the amethyst out of her hands when she'd fallen asleep and put it in the basket on her dresser.

Better to say, perhaps, that she turned her enormous copper-colored eyes toward his face and smiled.

But why his brain was quibbling about word choice, he had no damn clue.

"And I'm a painter," she said, yawning a little. Then she smiled. "It sounds like the title of a wonderful romance novel, doesn't it? The Painter and the Pirate. *Ooh.*"

She shivered a little, still smiling. "That sounds like a book I would buy definitely buy."

"You don't understand," he said bleakly. "I've done bad things. I break rules. I step out of lines. I'm uncivilized. I'm selfish and self-centered, and you deserve better."

She blinked, but said nothing. Then she blinked again.

Then she started to laugh.

Frustration was making his gut hurt. "Why are you laughing?"

"I was just thinking: The Painter and the Wicked Pirate. Oh my gosh, that sounds *way* sexier. I would totally read that."

He closed his eyes and thudded the back of his head against the wall. Once, twice, a third time. Then he groaned, long and loud. "Listen to me. You don't understand –"

She sat up very suddenly and swung one leg over both of his to straddle him, which effectively put an end to any speech he'd been about to make. Then she put her hands on his shoulders, slid them up to the sides of his face, and held his head still.

He stared into her beautiful eyes and waited for whatever she wanted to say. She had his *complete* attention.

"You listen to me, Pirate. I understand *everything*. I understand the man that you are probably better than you do. I understand that you could be off pirating or wenching or robbing helpless widows and kittens, but instead you sat here with me for hours, to be sure I was all right." She leaned forward and kissed his forehead, then his nose, then his right cheek, and then his left.

He held perfectly still. To move might break the spell.

She kissed his nose again and then drew one finger down the length of it. "You have a wonderful nose. I'd love to paint you sometime. Would you let me?"

His head was spinning, and he didn't know what to answer first. "My nose? What are you talking about? Widows and kittens? I don't think you're taking me seriously."

She made a funny little sound and then wiggled around on his lap, which drove all the blood in his body straight to his cock.

"You have a lovely nose." She moved her hands to the sides of his head again and shaped the outsides of his ears with her fingertips, which was possibly one of the most erotic things anyone had ever done to him.

Or else he was losing his damn mind.

"These are wonderful ears, too. You know, ears are so difficult to get right. So many people have ones that stick out in weird ways. You never think about an ear until you try to paint one, really," she said, as if confiding a great secret.

"I don't want to paint ears," he growled.

"I don't want to paint ears either," she said, looking surprised. "I want to paint all the bits of your body that are underneath your clothes. With long, slow strokes of my paintbrush. Dipping into special colors, gemstone-infused colors. Getting the light exactly right in the blue of your eyes and the golden brown of your skin—I'm imagining you have tan skin, I couldn't really tell—and the perfect, rosy blush color for the length of your long, hard—"

"Stop," he roared.

Rather than being intimidated, though, she laughed at him. A gentle, teasing laugh; one that made him want to taste every inch of her body. She leaned forward again; wiggled a little again.

He was almost certainly going to lose his mind, trying to keep from taking advantage of this woman.

"Oh please, Dare. Please take advantage of me," she said with a breathy little moan.

"I said that out loud?" He was losing it.

"Or maybe—just maybe—I can be brave enough to take advantage of you." She leaned down and touched her mouth to his gently, the barest impression of lips on lips. He held his breath, longing for and yet afraid of what she might do next.

She paused, though, and bit her lip.

"It's only... it's only that I've never actually seduced anyone before," she confessed. "I mean, I'm not a virgin. There were the mandatory college fumblings, but I've never —I don't—I'm probably not very good at this."

Suddenly, all her bravado seemed to drain away, and he was profoundly certain that he didn't want that to happen

"You're on the right path," he said hoarsely. "Try again. I dare you."

With that, he put his hands on her hips and pulled her even closer until she was snug against his body, but then he leaned his head back, closed his eyes, and sat perfectly still.

Waiting for a slightly wild creature to trust enough to touch him again.

For a long moment, she didn't move. Then tentatively, so tentatively, she moved forward and touched her lips to his. But this time, he was having none of that. He cupped the back of her head with one hand and deepened the kiss. Caressing, seducing, and tasting her mouth with his own. She moaned – or was that him?

It didn't matter. It was probably both of them. Kissing her was like nothing he'd ever experienced before. No simple matter of tongues and lips or even teeth; no sheer animal physiology and instinct. This was more—this was deeper. He felt like she was touching his *soul*.

Worse—he never wanted her to stop.

When she finally broke the kiss and pulled slightly away, gasping for air, he was panting, too.

"I have to have you, Lyric. You to know that, right?" He heard the husky growl in his own voice, but he couldn't seem to help it. Every nerve ending in his body was screaming at him to claim her. "Please say yes. Please, please say yes."

She shifted forward and kissed him again, and then a smile of surpassing sweetness spread across her face.

"Dare? I need—"

"Anything," he promised fervently. "*Anything*. Anything for you."

"I need to paint."

Within forty minutes her head was covered with tiny, close-lying curls that made her look wonderfully like a truant schoolboy. She looked at her reflection in the mirror long, carefully, and critically.

"If Jim doesn't kill me," she said to herself, "before he takes a second look at me, he'll say I look like a Coney Island chorus girl. But what could I do—oh! what could I do with a dollar and eighty-seven cents?"

At 7 o'clock the coffee was made and the frying-pan was on the back of the stove hot and ready to cook the chops.

Jim was never late. Della doubled the fob chain in her hand and sat on the corner of the table near the door that he always entered. Then she heard his step on the stair away down on the first flight, and she turned white for just a moment. She had a habit for saying little silent prayer about the simplest everyday things, and now she whispered: "Please God, make him think I am still pretty."

-- *The Gift of the Magi*, O. Henry (1917)

*L*yric was reconsidering her sanity.

She'd wanted this man in her bed and in her life for so long, and now she'd stepped away from him to *paint?*

"You're definitely losing it, Fielding," she muttered to herself.

But it was as if madness had caught her, captured her, carried her away on a tide of exploding creativity. The *colors.*

Oh my God, the colors. The garden. Dare himself. She needed to paint all of it.

She needed to paint, more than she needed her next breath. She didn't know how to explain that to him— she needed him, too. More than she'd ever needed anyone in her life. But the fever had her, more powerfully than it ever had before, and she had to answer the Muse.

"Dare, you understand, don't you? Please, please tell me you understand," she pleaded. She was already out of bed and cautiously feeling her way across the room to find her paints and easel. She needed her canvas like a junkie needed a fix, *right now right now right now.* She hoped he understood.

He *had* to understand.

Decidedly grumpy noises were coming from the direction of the bed, but she heard his feet hit the floor, and he walked over to her. "Let me help."

"I don't need—"

He touched her arm. "I know you don't need my help. But I need to give it. Can you allow me that, at least?"

She breathed him in, inhaling the scent of sea and spice and salt that was uniquely him. She wanted to paint him. A portrait. A nude. Once—*if*—she had the chance to learn every inch of his body, she would take that knowledge gained through sensory input, through the touch of her fingertips and lips and skin, and use it to paint him.

The irony, of course, was that she'd never be able to see the portrait. Adding irony to irony, there was even a name for what she did: blind contour drawing. It didn't refer to blindness, of course. If referred to the artist technique in which the artist concentrated solely on the subject of the drawing or painting, and never looked at her canvas while she worked.

She'd joked to Meredith once that *all* of her work was blind contour, but Meredith hadn't found it very funny. Her friend hadn't much of a sense of humor when it came to Lyric's blindness.

Dare. He'd asked her something...Oh.

"Of course I'll allow it," she said, placing her hand lightly on his arm. "I would love to have your help because you're offering it to me as a gift and not as an obligation."

He stopped moving, and she felt the muscles of his arm tighten just before he caught her mouth in a deep, claiming kiss.

When he finally released her, he lifted her chin with a finger. "Lyric, I'm a pirate. I don't do *anything* out of a sense of obligation. You should at least know that about me by now. Every single moment I've spent with you has been entirely and completely because I wanted to be here."

"I—oh." She didn't know what to say to that. It was a gift too large and too important for her to unwrap right now, caught in the throes of the Muse's demands. Instead, she pulled his head down to hers and kissed him again. She tried to put everything she felt – everything he meant to her —into the kiss, but how could that even be possible? A kiss was a single note, and her feelings for him were an entire symphony. She wanted so much for him to understand, to believe in her.

She wanted him to believe in himself.

"Although," she said, grinning mischievously, "I still think The Painter and the Wicked Pirate has a lovely ring to it."

He laughed his deliciously low, husky chuckle and then surprised her by smacking her on the butt. "Enough of this screwing around. We need to make some art happen. And when I say we, I mean you, because I can't draw—"

"—a straight line," she finished for him. "Yeah, I get that a lot."

So many of the non-artistic people in her friend group and the tourists who came into her studio had said some variation of that phrase to her over the years. Sometimes it was funny, and sometimes it was annoying, how they seemed to look at her as if she were a trained monkey in a zoo doing a particularly interesting trick. They'd hasten to tell her all about how they couldn't draw straight lines, or couldn't draw stick figures. And sometimes she had to clamp her jaw tight to avoid saying anything like:

Well, rulers are a thing.

Or

Who would want to draw a stick figure anyway?

Tourist dollars didn't flow into her studio because she was rude to the paying customers, though. She had to create; it was as important to her as breathing – but she also had to eat. And as long as people wanted to buy her paintings, she felt it was a wonderful bargain.

A little prep, and she was ready to channel whatever the Muse was sending. The gardens. It had to be the gardens. Not the gardens as she'd imagined them when they'd first walked through, but the vivid, impressionistic shapes and colors and light that she'd seen while holding the amethyst.

"Eat your heart out, Renoir," she muttered, clenching one paintbrush between her teeth while she selected another.

He moved to stand behind her and put his hands on her shoulders. "Do you like his work? Renoir?"

"Do I like his work? He's only one of the greatest painters of all time," she told him. "I could stand in front of *Bal du Moulin de la galette* for days. I was fascinated with it when my parents took me to Paris. Now I can only see it in my memory, but it will never fade."

"His great, great, I don't know, maybe 100-times great-grandfather was Atlantean."

She dropped her paintbrush. "What? Are you telling me —no. *Argh*. It has to wait. I want to hear that story. I want to hear a thousand of your stories, but right now I have to paint. I need to paint."

She heard his footsteps, and then the distinctive creaking sound of a large, muscular man sitting down in a wooden chair. "You need to paint, I get it. So I'll just sit here and watch."

Oh, that was so not happening. She turned her entire body in his direction and put on a stern face. Or least as stern of a face as she could manage just after she'd been licking the man's ear a few minutes before.

"No. I'm sorry, but I can't work with someone watching me. Not in the initial phase. Can you, I don't know, go do some Atlantean thing for a while?" She made little shooing motions with her hands, and he started laughing.

"Fine. I'll go do Atlantean things. But I'll be back, and I expect payment on what we started here tonight," he said, sounding only a little disgruntled.

She smiled but could feel the heat of a fiery blush

working its way up from her chest to her cheeks. "Oh, I can promise you that, Captain."

She heard his footsteps come closer again and then a thud next to her.

"I put a small side table here," he said, taking her hand and moving it to the table's surface. "I'm going to get you a glass of water, and then I'm going to leave and go do my Atlantean things. I'll also have some food sent up, since you missed dinner."

"Sure. Right. Later," she said, already too distracted by the insistent pulse in her head of the painting that she needed to create.

Blues. Blues and greens and whites. The marble of the palace; that would be tricky. But as a backdrop for the flowers—oh, if only she could capture the extraordinary bouquet of scents in those flowers. Nothing she'd ever smelled before, which made sense. After all, they were probably species of plants that hadn't been seen on Earth in millennia.

Greens. Reds—oh the pinks and purples, they'd shone so vividly in the vision she'd had while holding the jewel. Maybe she should begin with the fountain and center it on the page and focus the eye on the water. Flowing, dancing, sparkling: water like she'd never seen since before the accident. If she could capture the water...

If she could capture the water, she could capture the feeling.

She picked up a brush and began.

$\approx$

*L*yric woke up feeling drained. But in a good way. When she tried to sit up, however, she rolled right off the bed. When she hit the floor, she realized she'd been sleeping upside down with her feet on the pillows.

Well, it wasn't like that hadn't happened before. When she was in the middle of a creative burst, sleep, food, and sometimes even oxygen seemed unnecessary.

She made her way carefully to the bathroom, but it wasn't a problem because she'd fixed the dimensions of the room and placement of the furniture and doors in her mind earlier when she'd taken a brief break to use the restroom, splash water on her face, and try to shake out her cramped hand.

By the time she showered and was ready to face the day, she came out of the bathroom to a delicious scent of breakfast and coffee, and she followed her nose toward it. Someone had brought a cart and left it just inside the studio door. She appreciated the thought, and especially appreciated that they hadn't put it inside the bedroom door. She wasn't entirely sure how real palace servants acted, but the ones on TV and in books were always scurrying around, going in places where nobody wanted them to go. She hated the idea of people she couldn't see popping in uninvited to see her. For now, though, she just felt gratitude... and hunger.

"This is Atlantis, my friend. We have superior Atlantean coffee beans," she mumbled, carefully pouring herself a cup.

She'd just taken her first delicious sip of heavenly goodness, otherwise known as caffeine, when she heard someone walk into the room.

"Are you going to keep talking to yourself, or can anyone

join in the conversation?" The voice was female, one she hadn't heard before, and sarcastic as hell. Lyric was definitely not in the mood for snark before breakfast.

"I don't know," she said mildly. "I usually find that at least if I'm talking to myself, someone intelligent is listening."

There was a long moment of silence, and then the woman started laughing. "Well, you're not at all a meek little land mouse that Dare brought home to play with, are you?"

"I'm not a meek anything. Coffee?"

"I'd love some. Lots of sugar."

Lyric pointed toward the cart, not really wanting this rude stranger to watch her fumble around finding the sugar. "If you need so much sweetening-up, I'm sure you can do it yourself."

She heard the small clink of the spoon in the sugar bowl and then the sound of stirring. The woman dropped the spoon carelessly on the tray, and then silently sipped her coffee, giving Lyric time to form an impression.

The woman smelled like leather, oddly enough. Then she moved, and Lyric heard the slight *whoosh*—the rubbing noise of leather pants. Yikes. A badass, or so the woman wanted everyone to think.

Lyric rolled her eyes.

"I'm April. And you're Lyric Fielding. I didn't realize blind people rolled their eyes. It seems sort of ridiculous."

Wow. This woman was going for the jugular. And Lyric had no idea why, but in spite of not having had her first cup of coffee yet, the one thing she did know was that she wasn't going to let April No-Last-Name get to her.

"As delightful as it is to hear your observations on what blind people should and should not do, perhaps you'd like to get to the reason for this visit?"

April walked a few steps in a direction that Lyric definitely did not want her to walk.

"Stop," she told the woman sharply. "I don't share my
work when it's in progress, and I expect you to have the
courtesy to respect my wishes."

There was another small silence, but then April's footsteps approached Lyric again.

"Fair enough, mouse," she said. "So why are you here?"

Lyric was taken aback at the woman's bluntness, and
more than a little ticked off at her clumsy attempt at interro-
gation. "Well, I'd be happy to explain that to you, about ten
minutes after it's none-of-your-damn-business o'clock."

"Ouch. Well, I was headed to breakfast, and I happened
to walk by the room you're using as a studio," April said
blandly, lying through her teeth.

"Well, that's interesting," Lyric shot back." "Because to
my knowledge this room is on the corner of the east wing, so
there's no reason why you would just happen to be walking
by it unless you were headed here on purpose."

"Touché. Is that bacon?"

"It smells like bacon, but how would I know? Maybe
it's whatever passes for bacon from some weird Atlantean
pig."

April laughed, and Lyric had the feeling she'd surprised
it out of the woman. The manners that Aunt Jean had
pounded into her over the years raised their ugly head,
though, and Lyric sighed.

"Would you like some of my breakfast?"

"I know you just said that so I'd say no, but I'm going to
say yes. We should have a little chat," April said. "I'll pull up
some chairs."

By the time they finished eating a truly magnificent
breakfast, Lyric was no closer to understanding why April

had come to visit her. Finally, she put down her fork and decided just to get to the point.

"So why are you here? It's not just to share a random breakfast with a random visitor. So what is it?"

April made a little snorting noise. "I just wanted to get a look at you, all right? I wanted to see what Dare was bringing home these days. When he was with me, I thought he had a type. We sailed together, we smuggled together, we slept together. Life was an adventure every day of the week. But you. *You* I don't get."

Lyric could feel the steam building up in her head, ready to pour out her ears, but she stayed outwardly nonchalant. "If it was all that wonderful, why aren't you sailing with him now?"

"Oh we ran our course a few years back. Gods, I guess five years back now. But I'm in the mood for a little action. I thought I'd look him up."

Lyric poured herself another cup of coffee in silence, and then she smiled what Meredith called her sharkiest smile. "You can try."

It was a challenge, and they both knew it. She might not be a pirate, but she was sure as hell able to cross swords with this woman.

April laughed. "Unfortunately, I think I'm going to like you in spite of myself. Maybe I do see what Dare sees in you."

"I'm so relieved," Lyric drawled.

April shoved back her chair. "Well, when is he getting back? What did Poseidon say?"

The way she posed the question indicated that she expected Lyric to have the answer. Lyric suddenly realized, with a sick feeling in the pit of her stomach, that if she'd really meant anything to Dare, he would've told her about something so important as going in front of the— and she couldn't even believe she was going to think this—sea god.

Boy, times had changed.

She put down her cup and stood, too. "I'm sure he'll be back when he's done. Shall I tell him you stopped by?"

"No need. I don't have time to wait around until he gets finished with whatever he's doing with you, no offense."

Lyric narrowed her eyes. "I've found that usually when people say 'no offense,' they are saying something that is in fact *designed* to cause offense."

There was a silence, and then April made that small snorting noise again. "That was me shrugging. I just realized you couldn't see it, so I'm narrating. Sure, tell Dare I stopped by. Tell him it's his loss, and I'm going to join Denal in this new elite fighting team he's starting. So maybe I'll see him around, and maybe I won't."

"Elite fighting team?"

She could hear April heading for the door, but the footsteps stopped at her question. "Yeah. I'm going to be the first-ever of Poseidon's warriors to be female in the more than eleven thousand years since Poseidon first swore them into service."

Pride and something else—trepidation, perhaps?—rang in April's voice. In spite of herself, Lyric kind of wanted to wish her well. After all, that was one hell of a glass ceiling. eleven thousand freaking years.

"Good luck," she said impulsively.

"You really mean that, don't you?"

"Life is too short to say things you don't mean, don't you agree?"

April said nothing for a moment, but Lyric heard no footsteps to indicate she'd left yet, either. Finally, the woman replied. "Thanks. I hope I'm not going to need luck, but thank you anyway. You're more than I expected. I'd wish you luck, too, with Dare, but I'm not sure I'd really mean it. So instead, I'll just say see you around. And hey— tell Dare that I'm rooting for him. I know he feels like he's not whole on his ship without Seranth, because she's part of him, the ship, and even part of the sea itself. But he'd be bored to death on land. He can't give up the sea—he wouldn't. Not for anything—or *anyone*."

Lyric stood there, clenching her shaking hands into fists, for a long time after the sound of April's footsteps had faded.

Well. There was her answer. Even if Dare could love her, she'd bore him to death. So this little interlude in Atlantis meant nothing. Nothing would change between them. She'd continue to only see him a few times a year, until he ended up with someone like April.

What else was there for them? It wasn't like Lyric could become a pirate, even if she wanted to. Enough, already. She had work to do, and now she had an entire palette of new and unresolved emotions to use in the piece.

She walked over to her canvas and reached for the black paint.

10

The door opened and Jim stepped in and closed it. He looked thin and very serious. Poor fellow, he was only twenty-two—and to be burdened with a family! He needed a new overcoat and he was without gloves.

Jim stopped inside the door, as immovable as a setter at the scent of quail. His eyes were fixed upon Della, and there was an expression in them that she could not read, and it terrified her. It was not anger, nor surprise, nor disapproval, nor horror, nor any of the sentiments that she had been prepared for. He simply stared at her fixedly with that peculiar expression on his face.

-- The Gift of the Magi, O. Henry (1917)

Dare stood on the deck of the Luna, her bow pointed into the wind. He'd been sailing for hours, with a skeleton crew, calling out to Poseidon.

The thing about gods, however, was that they showed up when they felt like it. They answered your call if they felt like it, and sometimes not at all. Apparently, this was one of the times that Poseidon didn't feel like answering.

He'd sailed through the sunrise, even though he wanted with every fiber of his being to head back to port, head back to the palace, and climb into bed with Lyric. Or, if she were still painting, to sit quietly across the room. Not disturbing her, just watching her. Not intruding, just being part of her world.

But she was probably asleep, exhausted from the hurricane of painting she'd been so compelled to do. And he still had a goal to accomplish out here.

"Poseidon," he shouted. "Get your capricious sea god ass over here and talk to me about Seranth right now."

Behind him, Smitty gasped. "Captain! You're gonna get us killed. Don't you know better than to challenge the gods?"

Smitty wasn't even Atlantean, but like all other sailors, he had a healthy respect for gods, superstitions, and prevailing winds.

"No, he'll just smite me, if he's going to do any smiting. He's pretty fair, as gods go."

I AM GLAD TO HEAR YOU ESTEEM ME SO GREATLY. YOU KNOW HOW MUCH YOUR GOOD OPINION MEANS TO ME.

Poseidon's thundering voice made the mockery sound like cannon fire.

Dare realized he was in a lot of trouble.

"I need Seranth," he shouted up at the giant face floating in the sky above him. "You gave me *Luna*; now give me the sea spirit. You know I'm only half as fast and half as good without her, and what I do, I do for you and for the benefit of Atlantis."

WHAT YOU DO, YOU DO FOR YOURSELF. ANY EXTRA BENEFIT IS PROBABLY ACCIDENTAL AND CERTAINLY INCIDENTAL.

Behind Dare, Smitty dropped to the deck and covered his head with his hands. "Don't hurt me."

Dare gritted his teeth. "Poseidon. I ask this boon. Return *Luna* to me and Seranth to *Luna*. At least grant me that. You know she belongs with this ship—she's part of it. This must be hurting her even more than it hurts me, and I know that's not what you intended."

DO NOT PRESUME TO TELL ME WHAT I INTEND, PIRATE. YOU WILL ONLY ANGER ME, AND YOU WILL ALWAYS BE WRONG.

TAKE THE SHIP. YOU PAID FOR IT IN SWEAT, BLOOD, AND GOLD. I WILL NOT GIVE YOU THE SEA SPIRIT, HOWEVER. YOU DO NOT DESERVE HER.

Dare roared out his frustration and then smashed his fists down on the railing. "Without her, the ship alone is only half of my heart!," he shouted.

PERHAPS YOU LOOK FOR YOUR HEART IN THE WRONG PLACE.

And then Poseidon vanished.

Dare turned the ship around, the sea god's words ringing in his ears and in his mind. When he reached Atlantis, he headed straight for the tavern.

~

*I*t was mid-afternoon by the time the tavern owner'd had enough and thrown him out. Dare knew it had been a close call about half a bottle of whiskey earlier, when he'd broken that chair over somebody's head, but it was a hangout for lowlifes, after all, and he fit the bill.

He'd spent enough of his gold there over the years that it took more than a broken chair—or a broken head—to get him kicked out.

"And it's a broken heart that sent me here," he said, stumbling down the path toward the palace, full of expensive whiskey and expansive melodrama. Maybe a little self pity thrown in for good measure.

Without Seranth, he and *Luna* were just another pirate and ship, no longer the best on the high sea. *Looking for his heart in the wrong place...*

Without Lyric, what does it matter?

The thought knocked him sideways, and he stumbled and almost fell. Well, maybe it was the whiskey knocking him sideways, but the thought of life without Lyric...

He needed to talk to her. To explain—he wasn't exactly sure what he wanted to explain. That he needed her? That he didn't feel like he deserved her?

That he loved her?

He froze right in the middle of the path. He *loved* her?

Yes. By the gods, he *did* love her, and he knew she felt something for him. He tried to gather his alcohol-soaked wits to figure everything out logically, but it wasn't working because:

She was an artist, and she lived in Florida, where she had her home, her studio, and her business. All her friends were there.

And

He lived in Atlantis, and was sworn to Poseidon, the rat bastard of a sea god. He couldn't leave without breaking that oath, and the sea god was not known for kindness to oathbreakers. Dare would be dead before he could get the words out.

He could visit her...?

He shook his head. No, after having her in his arms, he knew that mere visits would never be enough.

Enough already with the agonizing. Was he a man or

was he a sniveling idiot? He needed to see her. He needed to talk to her.

But first, he needed some coffee.

⁓

*B*y the time Dare stopped at a different pub to pound down three cups of coffee and then made it to the palace, it was dusk. He heard singing coming from the throne room, and headed in that direction. Maybe Lyric would've come down for the songs. A wave of shame washed over him that he'd left her alone all night and day while he wallowed in self pity. Poseidon had just cause to refuse him Seranth, he finally admitted to himself. He'd taken his ship into dangerous waters and risked them all for nothing but profit, adventure, and greed.

If he couldn't be a better person and a better captain, he didn't deserve any of them. Not Seranth, not *Luna* and her crew, and certainly not Lyric.

Lyric, who was the light to his darkness. The beacon by which he'd steered his ship for the past several years, even though he hadn't known it at the time. He loved her.

He *loved* her.

He turned the corner into the throne room, and then stopped and stared at the sight before him. The king and queen were sitting on cushions in the middle of the floor, surrounded by children of all ages. The parents—at least he assumed those were the parents—were arranged around the edges of the room. The queen seemed to be telling the children a story about a town called Bethlehem.

Wait. He knew this story. Poseidon's warriors at the time had brought back the amazing tale of the birth of the Christ child.

"What's frankincense and myrrh, Your Majesty?" One of the smaller children had asked the question, but Dare could see that many of the others wore the same look of incomprehension on their faces, and he enjoyed listening to Queen Riley explain the story of the three kings and their gifts.

He couldn't see a clear path to get through to the staircase to Lyric's room, so he leaned back against a wall, drawn into the story. It was a story of hope and love, and ultimately of healing and forgiveness.

His throat tightened and he swallowed hard.

Love, hope, and forgiveness. As if drawn by a homing beacon, his gaze swept the room for a glimpse of the woman with whom he wanted to share all of this. Share his life.

There she was, standing on the other side of the room, her eyes closed and a faint smile on her face as she listened to Riley's story of the King of Kings. As soon as the story ended, in joy and grace, Dare made his way around the perimeter of the group with single-minded intent. He had to reach her. Nothing else mattered. He had to tell her—he had to explain.

He needed to make her love him back—whether he deserved her yet or not, he would vow to spend a lifetime trying.

11

D ella wriggled off the table and went for him.

"Jim, darling," she cried, "don't look at me that way. I had my hair cut off and sold because I couldn't have lived through Christmas without giving you a present. It'll grow out again—you won't mind, will you? I just had to do it. My hair grows awfully fast. Say `Merry Christmas!' Jim, and let's be happy. You don't know what a nice—what a beautiful, nice gift I've got for you."

"You've cut off your hair?" asked Jim, laboriously, as if he had not arrived at that patent fact yet even after the hardest mental labor.

"Cut it off and sold it," said Della. "Don't you like me just as well, anyhow? I'm me without my hair, ain't I?"

-- The Gift of the Magi, O. Henry (1917)

L yric smiled and chatted with the people near her after Riley's story was done. When the singing began, she joined in, figuring out the lyrics to the Atlantean children's songs as they went along. She loved to sing and wasn't going to let a little thing like not knowing the words stop her.

She closed her eyes and sang, letting the joy and companionship in the room soothe her soul and infuse her with the spirit of the season. In the middle of a song that seemed to be about fish and grapefruit, as far as she could grasp the meaning, she felt something Meredith would have called a disturbance in the force. It was as if the air pressure in the room changed; as if a powerful gale force wind were headed straight toward her.

Dare.

She could feel him. It didn't make sense, had never made sense, but there it was. She could feel him coming for her, and her body started trembling in spite of herself.

He stopped in front of her and pulled her into his arms. She could feel that he was trembling, too.

"I'm here. I'm back. I'm so sorry I left you alone for so long, but I never will again, I swear it."

She almost fell over. "You—what? Dare, are you—"

She stopped, not knowing how to finish her sentence. There had been April, after all. The adventurous, exciting April. How could he make promises about his future with her, when his past had held such different desires?

Even so, how could she refuse him? She'd tried guarding her heart. She'd tried for years.

His voice had had a strange lilt to it, so she leaned forward and sniffed. Sure enough, his 'important business' seemed to have taken him past at least one Atlantean whiskey distillery. She leaned back, unsure whether to be amused or annoyed, but amusement won out.

"Really? If you wanted to go drinking, I would've been happy to go with you."

"I would've asked you, but you threw me out so you could work," he said humbly.

She had to laugh. Dare and 'humble' didn't belong in the same sentence. "I know. You're right. I have the manners of a wild boar when the Muse takes me like that. I'm sorry too, but you're back now. Should we go for a walk? It's a beautiful night."

He grasped her wrist and started walking, pulling her none too gently along with him.

"Beautiful night, yes. No to walks. I have things to say to you, and I'd like to say them in private."

She stepped up her pace to keep up with him and twisted her wrist a little until she was holding his hand. "That works out well then, because I have things to say to you too."

The sound of the crowd had been fading steadily as they walked along, and suddenly Dare swung her around until her back was against one of the cool marble walls of the palace.

"I've changed my mind. I can't wait until we get up to your room. I need to put my hands on you." With that, he took her mouth in a deep, passionate kiss. His hands stroked down her back until he found her butt. He squeezed it and then lifted her up, startling her into wrapping her legs around his waist.

"*Dare*. What if somebody walks down this hallway?"

He tore his mouth away from hers, breathing hard. "I don't care," he growled. "Let them get their own damn hallway."

He flexed his hips so the hardness of his body was exactly in the spot where she wanted it, and she moaned and went boneless, clutching at his shoulders for all she was worth.

"Dare—"

He bit her neck.

She cried out. "*Please*. Please, let's go to my room. I would like to have this conversation with you, but I'd like to have it in private."

"Why didn't you say so?" He swung her up into his arms. "This will be faster."

She wrapped her arms around his neck and decided to bite *his* earlobe this time.

"You keep talking about my round butt, so I find it hard to believe you want to carry me up three double flights of stairs again."

"Ha. You weigh nothing. Remember, superior Atlantean strength."

By then, he was running up the stairs. Luckily they didn't pass anyone, or at least not that she heard, because it probably would've been entirely obvious what they were rushing off to do.

At least, what she *hoped* they were rushing off to do.

By the time they made it to her room, she was already ripping the buttons off his shirt.

He lowered her to her feet and took her face in his hands. "I need to tell you something."

"I need to tell you something too," she said.

"In this, I won't be a gentlemen. I need to go first." He took her hands and knelt on the floor. "I must tell you that I have finally realized why I've been living with a hole in my heart for so long—because you weren't with me. Lyric, I love you more than life itself. Without you, I have nothing, want nothing, and feel nothing. My soul is yours, my heart is yours, my life is yours. I will give you anything and everything you could ever desire, if only you'll be mine."

Lyric couldn't stand for him to be kneeling. She wanted

them to be equals, always. She pulled him to his feet again until he was facing her and then she began to speak, heedless of the tears running down her face.

"Is this even possible? How can this be happening to me? I've waited all my life for a Christmas miracle—I've always believed—even when my parents died. Even when the doctors told me I'd never see again. I always believed, and hoped, and waited. And now—*oh, Dare*—now *you* are my Christmas miracle. I love you, and I'll love you forever."

He kissed her then, and the world stopped spinning on its axis for a long, long time.

"I know your home is important to you," he said roughly when they finally pulled apart. "I would give up the sea for you, were you to ask me."

"I would never ask you to do that."

"No. You're right. I shouldn't ask you to make the choice. You don't have to ask. I renounce the sea for you on my own initiative."

She shook her head and backed away a step. "No. No, you can't –"

"Lyric. Are you trying to tell me that you won't have me?" His voice was rough, intense in a way she'd never heard before. "I won't accept it after you told me you love me. I don't want to need you more than air, or light, or life, but I do. You own me now, body and what's left of my blackened soul, and I'll never let you go."

"Then don't. Don't let me go," she whispered, and held out her arms.

When he stepped into her embrace, it felt like she was finally—*finally*—coming home.

And when their clothes and inhibitions fell away and he took her into his arms, she knew that forever had finally begun.

~

*D*are's control was disintegrating. Lyric stood before him, her skin shimmering ivory in the moonlight streaming in from the open doors to the balcony.

"Don't ever let me go," she repeated, and the words were a blessing and a benediction, permission and invitation.

He wanted her more than he'd ever wanted anything in his cold, lonely life, and yet now that she was in his arms, he was stunned speechless. Gulping in air, drowning again. Drowning in hunger, desire, and pure, primitive *need* so fierce and powerful that he was all but driven to his knees before it.

Some remnant of his conscience forced him to speak. "I can never be good enough for you," he rasped.

A smile filled with seduction and sheer feminine power slowly curved her lips upward. "Then be bad enough for me."

Dare's control buckled, trying to break free of the tight leash he held on it. "Now," he growled. "I need you *now*."

She slid her arms around his neck, and the feel of her lush breasts pressing against his chest drove him to madness. He crushed his mouth to hers, desperate to taste her. Desperate to claim her. To possess her.

She ran her fingers through his hair and cupped his face, kissing him back, pressing her body even closer to his.

He released her mouth and kissed his way down the side of her neck, letting his teeth scrape against the sensitive curve where her neck met her shoulder, and he was rewarded with a gasp and then a delightful little moan that made him even harder.

"More, more, more," she demanded, and then she bit his

earlobe and a spasm of electric desire clenched down low in his body.

"More," he agreed. "Now." He swept her up into his arms, and then he dropped her onto the soft bed and pounced. "I need you more than I need air to breathe. If you want me to stop, tell me now, because I don't know how long my sanity will survive your touch."

Her lips parted, and those beautiful copper eyes smiled up at him. "Don't stop. And you drive me crazy, too," she told him.

And then she touched him and he went mad. He licked the pulse in her neck, and she shivered in his arms. She was so delicate, so fragile. . . but no. Not delicate, not fragile. She was fearless and a warrior in her own right, conquering her life and her art and her naysayers.

She was *everything*.

She was *his*.

"You're trembling, too," she whispered, tracing her fingers down the muscles of his chest.

"I can't help it. Your touch is turning my control to ash. I need to touch every single bit of your body." He kissed a path down to her breasts, and finally, finally, put his hands on them. "So beautiful," he murmured. "Mine."

She made that breathy moaning sound again—the one that shot sparks straight to his cock. "Dare, I want . . . I want-
-"

"I want, too. So much." He kissed her breasts, each in turn, and then licked a nipple into his mouth and gently sucked on it, his fingers gently pinching its twin.

Lyric's body arched up off the bed and she reached out and clutched his shoulders. "Oh, my, oh, my, oh, my, touch me. Please, please touch me and kiss me, more and more," she whispered. "Let me touch you."

He gave her other breast the same attention, licking her erect nipple and then gently biting, just a little, to share the electric sensation that was sparkling and snapping through his body. He rubbed his thumb over the tip of her other breast, still wet from his mouth, and felt her writhe beneath him.

She stroked his body with her hands, first tentatively and then more boldly, and then one hand reached lower to explore, but he caught her wrist, groaning. "Oh, gods, I want your touch so much. But I can't. If you touch me now, I'll go off like an untried youngling, and I want tonight to be about you."

"About both of us," she whispered.

He'd never been so hard in his life, and he didn't know if he'd survive it. His cock was already hard as steel against her softness, and every moan, every gasp only made him harder. When her body jerked under his and she rubbed her hips against him, he wanted nothing more than to plunge into her right then. Thrust into her until she surrendered—take her body until she gave him her heart.

Until she screamed his name.

And then screamed it again.

Instead, he ran his hand over the softness of her belly and then down further, cupping her and testing her with his fingers, Exulting in the wetness he discovered there. He raised his head and kissed her again while dipping his index finger into her wet heat and then sliding it up and around and over the delicate bud of her desire. She cried out and dug her nails into his back, clenching her thighs together and squirming on the bed.

"Yes, Lyric. More. Give me more." He bent down to take her nipple and sucked, hard, while his fingers continued a pattern of stroking and circling that was causing Lyric to toss her head back and forth on the pillow. She was moaning and her breathing fractured into gasps and pants, and he loved every single sound.

He was making her moan for him.

He was going to make her come for him.

He drove two fingers inside her and plunged his tongue into her mouth with a rhythm older than time. "Come for me, Lyric. Come for me, now."

Her body stiffened and arched off the bed, and then she cried out, shuddering against him, clenching his fingers in her hot, wet heat and jerking her hips again and again. "Dare! Oh, I don't—I can't--"

"Yes, you can," he told her ruthlessly, and he moved down her body while she was still shuddering with her orgasm. He pressed her thighs open with his hands and licked right across her core, and she screamed.

"I can't, it's too much, I want--" Her voice was shaky, but she was caressing his hair and his face and then she tightened her hands on his head and lifted to his mouth.

"You can," he told her, triumphant again, and he licked the center of her pleasure, smiling against her when she cried out and dug her fingertips into his shoulders.

When he sucked on her, just *there*, drew her tiny bud into his mouth and sucked on it, her sweet, sweet honey bathed him and she went rigid and screamed his name, coming so hard her body shuddered and convulsed on the bed.

Slowly, slowly, he pulled his fingers back, wiped his face on the sheet, and crawled up her body until he was settled between her legs and could capture her mouth again while she panted and shook beneath him.

"I want you. So much," he confessed, barely able to get the

words past the pleasure and arousal and emotion choking him. If he couldn't have her, he truly thought he might die, but to die in her arms would make his entire lonely existence worthwhile.

"Dare. I need you now," she said, her voice husky, and his world made sense again. "Now. Inside me, now. I can't think, I can't breathe, I can't exist one more second without you inside me."

The universe froze in time--stopped moving forward for a moment that lasted an eternity and yet was over in less than a heartbeat, and Dare's control finally and completely shattered.

"Yes. *Now*." He plunged into her warm, wet, welcoming heat and threw his head back in triumph, in ecstasy, in pure, primal pleasure. Sensation exploded within him, taking him over the edge from arousal to a raging maelstrom of hunger, desire, and jagged, sharp-edged need.

This feeling—being inside her—to call this arousal was to call a hurricane a summer breeze. He roared out his pleasure in a wordless cry of triumph and claiming.

Nothing had ever felt so good in his entire life as being inside her body. She was *his*.

He was . . . home.

~

*L*yric felt *everything*. She felt the world kaleidoscope around her into shards of song and light and color; the heat of his strong, big body, all hard angles and curved lines of muscle and bone. He'd kissed her and she'd fallen; he'd touched her and she'd exploded; he'd put his mouth on her and she'd shattered.

Then he'd entered her and now she was flying apart into

a prism of emotion and desire and pure, crystalline sensation.

She'd touched him, too, touched all the places she'd longed to touch and taste for so very long. She wanted to paint him like this; she wanted time to imagine his body proud and nude and so aroused.

She *would* paint him. But not now.

Not *now*. Now thoughts of art and paint and canvas were meaningless. Now she was flame and desire; meeting him, stroke for stroke. Thrust for thrust. Frantic with need and hunger, desperate for more and more and more of the pirate in her bed and in her heart.

He kissed her with fire and possession and she felt wanted. Felt beautiful. Felt loved. Wanted him never, ever to stop. Never, ever to let her go.

"So wet for me, Lyric," he rasped, moving on top of her and inside of her, surrounding her with his heat and strength. "You're so wet, just like I knew you would be. I want to taste you again. I want to spend days and weeks tasting and caressing and learning every inch of your body."

"Yes," she moaned. "Yes to all of it, all of it, more and more and more."

Then he moved his hips against her, driving so deep into her she didn't know where she ended and he began, they were Lyric and Dare, a tornado of incandescent sensation, of pleasure and desire and need, and she lost the ability to speak, or think, or do anything but feel and feel and feel. . . her body tightened and tightened and rose higher and higher to a peak she'd just conquered moments before with his lips on her body.

"Oh my, oh my, how can I even, oh Dare. Dare," she whispered or shouted and she was exploding, her body was shaking apart into individual atoms of warmth and beauty and radiance even as she could feel his thrusts speeding up, harder and harder, his body desperate against hers.

"Come for me, Dare, my pirate," she whispered, and as if given permission he drove so deep inside her that he surely touched her soul and then he shuddered, his body clenching and his hips pulsing as he exploded inside her.

"Lyric," he cried out, and she could feel him all around her, could feel him in her heart in a blaze of heat and flame and *knowing,* and then suddenly, with no warning at all, she could feel him in her soul.

The room swirled around them, faster and faster, and she clung to Dare. Her mind collapsed and reformed and expanded again, and she realized that this was a vision, not reality.

A vision of Dare as a child.

Dare crouching in shadows, in a barn? Stables? Shrinking back from a blow...

Flash.

Dare climbing the rigging on a ship, maybe a teenager? Falling, hitting the deck so hard she cried out even though she knew it wasn't happening now...

Flash.

Dare on a bigger ship, a graceful ship with clean lines and a winged figurehead. Standing at the bow with an ethereal figure who must be Seranth...

Flash.

Dare, on the ship, in taverns, in fights, in danger, alone, alone, alone, always alone...

Flash.

Dare walking into her gallery that first time. She gasped to see what it looked like and felt a fierce pride in the sight of her paintings hanging on the walls. *She* had created those.

She'd made that art. She shared his appreciation for her work and it warmed her, body and soul.

"Is that a cat, or a footstool with feet?"

Flash.

She felt him now, watched him walk away from her gallery, from St. Augustine, from her, and felt his regret. Watched years spin by as regret turned to longing, longing turned to sorrow. Yearning turned to . . . love?

Love? He loved her?

Flash.

His despair when he went overboard, his contentment when he woke up in her bed, his joy at bringing her to Atlantis, his . . .

Love.

She closed her eyes and waited, holding Dare like her life depended on it, while the magic pulled her inside his soul and then returned the favor and deposited him inside her. Flashes of memory, the music of constellations, lights and rainbows and darkness and radiance swirled around and through her, through him, through both of them, drawing them together even closer, binding golden thread through the tapestry woven between them over the past six years. She smelled a sharp, clear scent, so familiar. Sea and salt and Dare.

She laughed, but felt tears on her cheeks; she wept but knew she smiled. She held him and kissed him and waited, wondering and awed, for the room to stop spinning, and then she rested her head against his chest and inhaled all the air that she hadn't been able to breathe for who knew how long.

"Lyric? Lyric, please tell me you're okay," he demanded, and the love and concern and just...*Dare* in his voice answered all the questions she never needed to ask. She raised her head and put every ounce of her love for him into her smile.

"You love me," she told him. It wasn't a question. Not anymore.

"I do," he admitted, tightening his arms around her and kissing her forehead. "And you love me. The truth can't hide from the soul meld."

"I do," she agreed, still smiling. "But you didn't need the soul meld to learn that. You must have known."

"I didn't dare to hope. Give me a day or two to be my usual arrogant self, and I'll say of course I knew, but here and now, in this room, in the aftermath of that, I've only got honesty for you," he rasped.

A sudden thought caused her heart to clench in her chest. "You didn't. . . you haven't done the soul meld with anyone else?"

He rolled over in the bed, pulling her with him so they lay on their sides facing each other, their legs intertwined. "Never. That is an experience that few are ever lucky to have, and those who do only find it with one person in a lifetime. One love. You."

"A lifetime is a very long time." She bit her lip. "Are you sure--"

"Lyric," he interrupted her gently, his voice hoarse. "You are as beautiful inside as out. I've never felt such light and joy and kindness. You are everything I never knew I needed, and I'm never going to let you go."

She tightened her arms around him. "I feel exactly the same way, my pirate."

He drew a breath. "Your accident. I saw it. Your parents. I'm so very sorry. If only--"

She reached up and found his lips with her fingers. "No.

Not tonight. No sadness or sorrow or regret. Just love. Just us."

"Just us," he promised. "I love you."

"Then kiss me again," she said, pulling him close.

So he did. He kissed her, and she melted into his embrace. He kissed her, and gave her himself, Atlantis, and the whole wide world.

He kissed her, and she finally came home, to her very own Christmas miracle.

J im looked about the room curiously.

"You say your hair is gone?" he said, with an air almost of idiocy.

"You needn't look for it," said Della. "It's sold, I tell you—sold and gone, too. It's Christmas Eve, boy. Be good to me, for it went for you. Maybe the hairs of my head were numbered," she went on with sudden serious sweetness, "but nobody could ever count my love for you. Shall I put the chops on, Jim?"

Out of his trance Jim seemed quickly to wake. He enfolded his Della. For ten seconds let us regard with discreet scrutiny some inconsequential object in the other direction. Eight dollars a week or a million a year—what is the difference? A mathematician or a wit would give you the wrong answer. The magi brought valuable gifts, but that was not among them. This dark assertion will be illuminated later on.

-- The Gift of the Magi, O. Henry (1917)

*L*yric woke up slowly, swimming toward the surface of consciousness in a lazy, meandering way. She felt warm and content and utterly, blissfully happy. The man in bed with her murmured in his sleep, and she remembered exactly why she felt so content.

The soul meld.

When they'd made love...it had been magical. Extraordinary. Music and color and light and *feeling*—oh, the feeling of his hard body fitting itself to the softness of her own. Silken, sensual, seduction beyond her wildest dreams. He was a man who took and took and took—every ounce of response she could give—and then gave back even more, until she'd screamed his name and soared into the stratosphere.

And then there had been even more.

He'd gasped and she'd felt...everything. She'd felt *everything*. She'd seen inside his soul, and he'd seen inside hers. She knew him now like she'd never known another person, *ever*, in her life. He'd opened his shields and let her see the lonely child—the battered adult—the pirate who threw himself into a dangerous sea to try to save the lives of a magical pair of very special animals. His bond with Seranth. And then...

Then she'd seen his love for her. It suffused every part of him with a golden glow. She saw how he saw *her*; how strong and beautiful she was in his eyes, and she'd fallen in love with him all over again.

The thing about the soul meld... he'd seen her, too.

And he'd said her name with such love. Such reverence.

When they'd made love again with their hearts open to each other—their *souls* open to each other—the experience had transcended anything that poets or artists or writers could ever capture. They had truly been melded into one, and she'd almost been afraid she'd shatter with the perfection of that moment.

Now, waking in his arms, the logical part of her felt like perhaps she should've been afraid of such intimacy, such a deep connection. She'd been alone and self-sufficient for so long. Was it too much, too soon? The soul meld was the deepest possible connection, but was it a shorthand for the years of getting to know another person that human relationships entailed?

But did it really matter?

She thought back to the jewel tones of the inside of Dare's soul. This man—this strong, brave, wonderful man. No, it didn't matter. All that mattered was that they'd found each other and would never, ever be apart.

Dare tightened his arms around her and started kissing the back of her neck, and she smiled, relaxing back against him. She loved him, and he loved her. That was the basic truth from which everything else would flow.

Nothing was easy, of course, even in a magical place like Atlantis. They had so much to figure out between them. But she knew that they could figure it out. They had love. They had understanding. They had—

"Let's go see some unicorns."

Lyric bolted upright, pulling the sheet up to cover her breasts.

"What? Is that some weird Atlantean euphemism?" Her cheeks heated up. "I mean, I'm totally in the mood for. . . if you are, but 'go see some unicorns' is a new one for me."

There was a moment of silence, and then he started laughing and drew her back down into his arms. "No. Although, yes. Definitely yes. But then after, let's go see some actual unicorns."

"What—"

But then he was kissing her, and the kisses deepened, and the sheet was suddenly gone from between them, and all thoughts of unicorns and other mythical creatures left her mind entirely.

~

She brought the amethyst with her when they left the palace, and he could tell from her short, quick breaths that she was hopeful and afraid all at once, but this time the jewel was just a jewel, and no further flights of vision or fantasy, or recurrence of euphoria, captured her this time. She slipped it into her pocket with a rueful smile.

He thought she didn't know whether to be devastated or relieved, and he found himself caught up in equally conflicting emotions. He didn't want the magic of Atlantis to consume her, but he knew the moments of sight had been a wonderful gift.

"It might happen again," she finally said, raising her shoulders a little and then letting them fall. "But even if it never does, I had that one rare moment, and I'll cherish it in my memories forever."

Her courage astounded him. Humbled him. He was meant to be the strong one. The warrior. And yet she stood ready to experience everything life had to offer, even risking her heart with pirate.

He'd never wanted her more.

He kissed her; he could do nothing else. He drew her to him, slowly so she could protest if she wanted to deny him, but then shouted a laugh of pure triumph when she melted against him and put her arms around his neck.

"We could go back upstairs," he rasped, when he could catch his breath.

She laughed and pulled away. "Not a chance, buddy. You promised me unicorns."

"We have basilisks, too," he told her. "You'd be one of the few who would be allowed to enter the enclosure, actually, because they couldn't turn you to stone, since you can't--"

He stopped short, furious at his own blunder, but she smiled and shook her head. "It's okay. Kind of fascinating, really. Maybe after the unicorns?"

"Sure." He took her hand in his and started walking, but she didn't move. "Lyric?"

She started to laugh, and he closed his eyes and simply stood there listening to the lovely sound of chiming bells in her voice.

"Dare? I know this is all normal life for you, but I just said 'we can visit the basilisks after we see the unicorns.' Out loud." She started laughing again. "My life is now a fairy tale."

He frowned, but then remembered she couldn't see his expression. "The Fae tales are almost all grisly and bloody and dire. Why would you compare our time here with those?"

"Oh." She abruptly stopped laughing. "No, not...not like the Grimm tales. Not chopping off feet and eating children. Like Cinderella and charming princes and that kind of fairy tale."

Bitter heat seared through him and it took him a moment to recognize it as jealousy. He'd never been jealous before. The realization took him off guard, but still. He didn't like how this was going.

"The princes are married," he said coldly, and then he

blinked when this comment drew another peal of laughter from her.

"No, silly man. *You* are my Prince Charming," she told him. "Only you."

So then of course he had to kiss her again. By the time they made it to the stables, he was so aroused he wanted to throw her onto the nearest hay bale, strip her bare right then and there, and plunge into her heat.

Instead, he thought desperately of cold streams, cold showers, icy rivers, and anything else that might help his pants fit less painfully.

"We're here," he told her, guiding her into the front entrance.

"What is that—I smell horses," she told him. "Don't think you're going to fool me into believing a horse is a unicorn. There *is* one significant difference."

He laughed. "No. We're going to ride the horses to see the unicorns."

Lyric pulled her hand out of his and folded her arms across her chest. "You're out of your mind."

"Quite likely," he admitted, thinking back over the events of the past few days. "But that has nothing to do with horses or unicorns."

"I can't ride a horse."

He took her hand again and walked her the few short paces to Honey's stall. "This is my favorite mare. She's gentle and calm. Here. Hold out your hand so she can sniff you, and then stroke her neck, firmly but gently."

Lyric's breath caught when Honey's breath snuffled out and then again when he placed her hand on the mare's neck.

"Oh, she's so silky soft," Lyric murmured.

"She likes you." Dare smiled at Lyric's reaction. Clearly

she liked Honey as much as the mare seemed to like her. "You see? You can ride a horse. Here. Give her this apple, but hold it out on your palm flat like this."

She understood at once when he smoothed her fingers open so that her palm lay flat, turned up, and he put the apple from the bin near the door onto her hand. She murmured meaningless compliments to the horse, who was delighted to get a treat from a new friend.

"She does like me!" Lyric's face lit up, and she stroked the mare's long neck.

"Of course she does." Dare closed his eyes and took a deep breath. To most, the scents of the stables would be something to avoid, but to Dare they were familiar and comforting. He'd fled to the horses whenever his family became too much to bear: his father's carousing that brought shame to the entire family, his mother's drunkenness and flirting, his brother Flynn's wildness, Liam's "perfect son" status.

And his own wildness. No good kid ever grows up to be a pirate, he reminded himself bitterly.

Here, though, in the stables, he'd learned to find a measure of peace. Old Grissont had tried to throw him out twice, but when the stable master had found Dare there a third time, beaten black and blue by his drunken father for some perceived infraction, Dare had mustered all the defiance he had left and told Grissont that he was meant to be a stable master one day, and he might as well start then.

The old man had stared long and hard at Dare's bruises and at the blood trickling down his face from his broken nose, and then he'd said he figured he needed a stable hand. Wondered out loud if Dare might know anybody who wanted the job.

"Three squares and a cot, and more hard work than you'll be

able to stand, at least at first, boy, but nobody will raise a hand to
you here."

He'd kept his word, too. When Dare's father, on a truly record-breaking bender, had come around to the stables with fire in his eyes and a whip in his hand, bellowing for Dare, Grissont had broken the man's arm.

Years later, when Dare's father died, not one of his sons attended his memorial service. Not even Liam, by then one of Poseidon's Warriors.

When Grissont died, Dare had been at his bedside.

Family was what—and who—you made it. His gaze arrowed to Lyric, who might not realize yet that she was his new family. She'd learn. She'd stay with him.

Something in his chest ached. *She had to stay with him.*

"You might be insane," Lyric said, stroking Honey's silky neck.

The mare stretched her head out to reach for the apple Lyric held on her palm.

"I'm not sure horses can be insane," Dare said, saddling his gelding. "Plato comes close sometimes, but in the end they're all about food, comfort, and a nice trot in the fresh air."

"Your horse is named Plato?"

"Inside joke."

Lyric gasped then made a delightful sound that was perilously close to a giggle when Honey delicately took the apple from her. "She likes me."

"Of course she likes you. Everybody likes you. You're amazing. In fact, you're so amazing that I am tempted to fulfill a certain teen fantasy of mine about tossing a beautiful woman down onto a hay bale and having my wicked way with her."

She sent a deliciously seductive smile over her shoulder

in his direction. "My wicked pirate. I just bet you had many women in the hay bales."

He shuddered at the thought of the old stable master catching him with him pants down like that. "Trust me, you're the first."

"But Dare, I can't ride a horse," she said, her voice turning serious. "You know that. I can't see to guide her, and—"

"Lyric."

"She'll be floundering around—"

"Lyric."

"What?" There was a lot of impatience in her voice, and she narrowed those beautiful copper eyes.

"*Honey* can see."

"But…oh. *Oh.* Really?"

"Really. She'll stay with Plato. They're old friends. So you'll stay with me. I won't let you fall, and Honey isn't about to stumble or take off sprinting, or fall into the ocean. You'll be fine."

Lyric's entire face lit up as if a million suns were shining through it. "Truly?"

"Truly."

"Then what are you waiting for? Help me onto this horse already!"

$\sim$

*L*yric felt every motion Honey made transmit from her legs and hips through her nervous system and straight into her heart. She was surrounded by sensation and loving every second of it. The warm feel of the mare beneath her and the silky feel of her skin and mane. The scent of horse and stable. The sounds—so many sounds. Dare's voice, their horses' steps, birds singing secrets to each other from the trees along the sides of the path. Even the faint roar of the ocean, not so very far away.

The feel of the cool breeze and the hot sun, and Dare's occasional touch on her arm.

"This is the best Christmas present I've ever had," she blurted out, when he was in the middle of describing a particularly bright flowering bush to her.

"It's not over yet. I have something else I want you to see—experience," he said, and she could hear the chagrin in his voice. "I'm sorry. It's surprising how many times I use 'see' or 'look' without thinking about it."

She shrugged carefully, still wary of moving around too much on the horse. "It's normal. Don't worry about it. What did you want me to experience?"

Just then, a startling noise like a crow's caw crossed with a donkey's bray sounded very nearby; ahead of them on the left.

Dare started laughing. "Well, they certainly don't sound as ethereally delicate and beautiful as they look, but we'll get you close and ask them if you can touch them."

"Ask who? Touch what?" She gritted her teeth. "Dare. Tell me now."

"The Siberian unicorns. What else?"

"Oh. Sure. What else?"

She heard the light thud of his feet as he dismounted, and then Dare helped her down off Honey, stealing several kisses in the process, and then he led her forward until she touched a huge, flat boulder.

"Let's sit here and see if they want to visit," he said quietly. "They went through a lot on the ship. They might not want anything to do with me."

"Are they…guests? Cargo? I don't exactly understand."

She tilted her head until she felt the sun's warmth on her face.

A soft nicker sounded from in front of her.

"They've decided to say hello. This is the female, Jane. She's maybe as tall as your head at her shoulder, and she's pure white from head to tail," he murmured. "Her mate, Bingley, is a good bit taller, and very protective. He's hanging back right now, looking like he'd be happy to bite me. Must not have forgiven me for that dip in the ocean, hmm, old fellow?"

"Jane and Bingley? Somebody is a *Pride and Prejudice* fan." She smiled and then inhaled sharply when she felt a velvety nose nudge at her hands. "Quick! Give me another apple."

A moment later, Dare put an apple in her hand and she held it out to Jane, palm flat the way he'd shown her in the stables. The unicorn gently took the fruit and chomped it down in a couple of bites, then nudged at Lyric again.

Lyric slowly and carefully lifted her hand, pausing partway. "Is it okay to touch her?"

"I'm guessing yes, since she'd the one who initiated the contact," Dare said. "Slow and gentle, okay?"

"Okay." Slowly she lifted her hand to right about the nostrils snorting warm breath on her face, and then she touched the soft nose. To her surprise, Jane pushed her nose into her hand, as if asking for more.

"She likes you, too," Dare said, amusement rich in his voice. "You may as well give it up, Bingley. It's hopeless. We're all under her spell."

"Oh, hush," Lyric told him, stroking Jane's nose. "You're—oh!"

She'd leaned forward, and a hard, pointed end poked her in the forehead. "Is that—"

"Yep. Unicorn," Dare said. "Didn't you believe me?"

She gently ran her hand up the creature's nose to the horn and then traced its length with her fingertips. "I walked through a magical portal with a pirate to the mythical lost continent of Atlantis, so I guess you could say I kind of took 'Siberian unicorn' on faith."

"We're not lost any longer," Dare pointed out, reasonably enough, and it made her laugh.

A low, grumbling noise alerted her to Bingley's presence, and she turned her face toward Dare. "Is he dangerous? Should I stop touching Jane?"

"Actually, I think he might be wanting to say hi, himself."

For a few magical seconds, Lyric found herself petting two unicorns at the same time, and then the animals apparently decided they had something else to do and trotted off.

Lyric's heart was filled with butterflies, fluttering in her chest with an overwhelming sense of joy and wonder. "I can't . . . I can't even tell you how I feel right now. That was incredible. This whole day has been incredible. Thank you."

She held out her hand, and Dare took it in his, raised it to his mouth, and kissed her fingers.

"Especially this morning. Incredible," he said, his voice husky.

She couldn't help it. She had to kiss him. She pulled his face down to hers and spent several lovely moments holding her pirate in the bright sunshine of an Atlantis day, next to the Siberian unicorns.

Bubbles of happiness---and astonishment—floated through her like champagne in a crystal flute. Christmas and miracles and joy and love. It didn't seem possible that all of this could be happening to her.

"It *is* happening, though," she whispered. "You're here, and you love me."

"Well," he pointed out, "you love me, too."

"Always. Tell me about them. Jane and Bingley."

Dare tightened his arm around her and dropped a kiss on her forehead.

"It's just that I needed to know they were okay." She felt his shoulder rise in a shrug. "I used my share of what was left of the cargo to buy them, and we found them this place near Mt. Atlantis to be their home. They seem to love it here, and their new caretaker is delighted."

"Dare! The wicked pirate has a heart, after all," she teased him.

"You *are* my heart," he said roughly. "You can never leave me, or I will be without a heart and a danger to all around me."

"I won't leave you, but—"

"But?"

"Maybe we could go back to the palace now and 'go see the unicorns' in an entirely different way," she said, blushing but not caring. She wanted him, and she was fiercely glad to be able to show him how much.

Little more than an hour later, they were tearing at each other's clothes even before they made it inside her door.

13

J im drew a package from his overcoat pocket and threw it upon the table.

"Don't make any mistake, Dell," he said, "about me. I don't think there's anything in the way of a haircut or a shave or a shampoo that could make me like my girl any less. But if you'll unwrap that package you may see why you had me going a while at first."

White fingers and nimble tore at the string and paper. And then an ecstatic scream of joy; and then, alas! a quick feminine change to hysterical tears and wails, necessitating the immediate employment of all the comforting powers of the lord of the flat.

For there lay The Combs—the set of combs, side and back, that Della had worshipped long in a Broadway window.

Beautiful combs, pure tortoise shell, with jeweled rims—just the shade to wear in the beautiful vanished hair. They were expensive combs, she knew, and her heart had simply craved and yearned over them without the least hope of possession. And now, they were hers, but the tresses that should have adorned the coveted adornments were gone.

But she hugged them to her bosom, and at length she was

able to look up with dim eyes and a smile and say: "My hair grows so fast, Jim!"

-- *The Gift of the Magi,* O. Henry (1917)

"*D*are." She let out a breathless laugh and pulled the heavy amethyst out of her pocket and placed it on a side table. "I think unicorn sightings are an aphrodisiac or something—"

But his fingers had stilled on her waist. "What in the nine hells is happening?"

"What do you mean?"

"That." His hand moved and she had a sneaking suspicion that he was pointing something out to her.

She sighed. "Really? *That?* After all these years? Maybe point less, talk more."

Dare drew a deep breath. "I'm sorry. I'm an idiot. This just caught me off guard. There's suddenly a very strong beam of light shooting up from your amethyst."

"A beam of light," Lyric repeated, feeling stupid. "I don't —what could that be?"

He pulled her toward him and gave her a quick but enthusiastic kiss. "I don't know, but no time like the present to find out."

Then he kissed her again, but this time he took his time. "Maybe we forget the gemstone and weird lights and I just take you to bed," he said in a husky growl.

"I—should we—" A delicious sensation shivered up her spine. She didn't know whether she was aroused, dazed, or both. She pulled her now-completely unbuttoned shirt closed and moved his hand off her butt. "Strong beams of light are not normal, even for Atlantis, I think. I mean, I had that in my pocket all afternoon. Any idea what it means?"

Dare whistled, long and low. "Not a clue. I've had it for years and years and years, and the amethyst has never done anything like this."

"What is it doing?" She was consumed by curiosity crossed with a hefty dose of impatience. "Tell me already!"

"I'm picking it up now. It's, *ouch*. Damn. The—"

"*Dare*. The rock? What ouch?"

"Right. It's pulsing with light, directing a pretty strong beam—oh, Poseidon's balls."

Lyric heard him mutter a string of what sounded like English mixed with Atlantean cursing.

"What happened?"

"It burned my fingers again, but before that, it told me what it is."

She heard him cross to the bathroom and then the sound of running water, so she followed him. "Are you badly burned?"

"No, it's nothing. I just wanted to run a little cold water on my fingers. It's a Wish."

Lyric was confused. "What do you mean it's a wish? Whose wish?"

"I don't know much about it or how it works. I just now that it's old. Not even old as much as ancient. Older than Atlantis. Older maybe than the gods. We have stories of Wishes— that's wish with a capital W—in our histories, but no one alive today has ever seen one. According to the old stories, they lie around disguised as other things,--apparently like gemstones—until they want to reveal themselves."

Lyric reached out for his arm. "What does it do, already?"

She felt him shrug. "It's exactly what it sounds like. It's a

Wish. According to the stories, it presents itself to a person whom it considers to be worthy. That person then gets to make one wish. *Any* wish. There's a legend that a stable boy was once king of Atlantis for a year and a day after he found a Wish." Dare laughed. "Hell of a story. No idea if it's true."

"That's true of all the best stories," Lyric said, smiling. "What are you going to wish for?"

He turned and pulled her close, dropping a kiss on the top of her head. "Oh no, *mi amara*. The Wish isn't here for me. It told me. It's here for you."

Her mouth fell open. "It's what? And what do you mean, it told you?"

"It's here for you," he repeated, excitement in his voice. "Lyric, you can wish for your sight!"

Ice coated her skin with cold fingers.

So fast.

He'd come to that conclusion so very fast.

She pulled away from him. "So what you're telling me is that I'm not enough for you the way I am now. You want to fix me, too."

It wasn't a question. More of a statement, really. A realization. She'd been deceiving herself—she'd been a fool. "Look, Dare. If you—"

His arms came around her like steel bands, and he swung her up into them and carried her across the room and tossed her on the bed. Before she could think, or breathe, or protest, he was on top of her, holding her face in his hands.

"If you really think that, you haven't been paying attention," he said roughly, just before he took her mouth with his. "You're not *enough* for me. You're *everything* to me. You are the star that guides me and I will never, ever let you go. I love you. Exactly. The. Way. You. Are."

And then he proceeded to prove it to her, slowly and very, very thoroughly, for the next few hours, until a knock at the door called him to a meeting with the king.

"I'll be right back," he promised, kissing her again. "We'll figure out the Wish later."

"I'll be here," she promised, snuggling deeper into the blankets. "Bring food."

He laughed. "As you *wish*."

She opened one eye. "Hey. Did you just Princess Bride me?"

His footsteps stopped. "Inconceivable!"

And then he was gone, and she sank back down in the pillows and thought that this might be the most hedonistic way anybody had ever spent Christmas Eve in the history of time.

Then she sat bolt upright in the bed.

It was Christmas Eve!

And the painting—her gift to Dare—wasn't finished.

Time to get to work.

～

L yric painted and painted with every ounce of emotion she'd felt during the time since she'd first come to Atlantis, and everything she'd felt for Dare for so long –the six long years that had led up to this moment.

She was possessed. The Muse was riding her. Driving her. This would probably be the best painting she'd ever done, and yet she suddenly knew it wouldn't be enough.

He loved her.

He *loved* her.

He'd offered to *give up the sea* for her. How could she give him only a painting, even the best painting of her life? No. She needed to give him something else. Something more.

This was Dare. This was the man she loved more than life itself and would love for eternity. He deserved the best gift that anyone had ever given, and she knew exactly how to get it.

She put down her paintbrush, walked carefully to the table, and felt for the amethyst. The Wish. Warmth surged into her skin, emanating from the large round stone. He'd said it 'told' him, but how did a rock tell anybody anything?

When it spoke to her, its voice sounding inside her mind, she was startled so badly she nearly dropped it.

Yes, I'm yours. I'm your Wish. Use me as you will.

The voice was tantalizing, and she spared a moment to wonder about the stories of all those who'd come before her in the thousands and thousands of years since the Wish had first come to be.

But it was Christmas Eve, and she had no time for wondering or stories or imaginings. She needed to make a wish—and for that, she needed to call Poseidon.

Lyric clutched the Wish in one hand and cautiously felt her way to the balcony that ran the length of the bedroom and adjoining room Riley had given her. She hadn't spent much time on it because she'd been at her easel so much. But it faced the sunset, Dare had told her, and she knew that if the sea god would be anywhere, he would be presiding over the sun setting across the waves of his ocean. She grasped the railing with one hand and held the Wish out on her palm with the other.

"Poseidon, I'm calling you. I don't exactly know how this goes, and I have the highest respect for you and your warriors. In fact, I'm choosing one of them—one of yours—for my own. He's why I'm calling you. Please hear my call."

She felt a little silly, but the Wish was whispering in her ear, so she repeated its words: "Poseidon, I invoke the power of the Wish. Please come to me now."

WHAT DO YOU ASK OF ME, HUMAN? aND WHAT-EVER IT IS, DO YOU REALLY THINK DARE IS WORTH IT?

She raised her chin in defiance, sparing a brief thought for how much she would have liked to actually see Poseidon's face. That would've been some story to tell Meredith when she went back to Florida to pack up her studio and retrieve her cat.

Oh, well. Dare could describe it to both of them.

"Poseidon, by the power of this token, I ask to exchange my Wish for Dare's sea spirit bond with Seranth to be whole again."

YOU ARE A VERY FOOLISH WOMAN. YOU COULD HAVE ANYTHING IN THE WORLD. ANYTHING FOR YOURSELF. VAST RICHES. POWER. YOUR SIGHT. AND YOU ASK FOR THIS? FOR THAT SCOUNDREL?

"He's *my* scoundrel." She smiled fiercely, even though she felt a few tears rolling down her cheeks. "I don't want riches, or power, or anything else but this. I only want Dare. And I exchange this Wish freely, because Dare *is* my Christmas miracle. He gave me his whole heart, and I want to give my whole heart back to him."

I HOPE HE CAN DESERVE YOU, WOMAN. VERY WELL. I HAVE NO CHOICE BUT TO AGREE. THE MAGIC OF THE WISH IS FAR OLDER THAN MINE.

A cool wind circled her body, twirling up from her feet and then around and around her until it rose past her head and vanished. When the wind was gone, she realized that the heavy weight of the Wish was gone, too. When she wrapped her fingers around the object that had taken its place on her palm, she could tell by the size and shape that it must be the copper band that symbolized Dare's spirit bond with Seranth.

Poseidon had fulfilled his part of their bargain.

Joy filled her soul until she almost worried that she might float right off the balcony. She'd seen inside Dare's soul; she'd seen his love for her and his longing for the sea. There could be no better gift for this man—*her* man.

And it was Christmas Eve—a time for miracles. Now all she had to do was wait. And perhaps she'd finish that painting after all and give it to the queen. Because a little Christmas magic had come her way from Riley, too. She walked back into her room, absolutely incandescent with happiness, and wrapped the armband in a scarf and put it under her pillow.

Her only tiny regret was that she wouldn't be able to see the joy on Dare's face when she gave it to him. She'd feel it, though, in his arms. *Oh*, how she'd feel it.

And that, after all, was the most important gift of all.

14

And then Della leapt up like a little singed cat and cried, "Oh, oh!"

Jim had not yet seen his beautiful present. She held it out to him eagerly upon her open palm. The dull precious metal seemed to flash with a reflection of her bright and ardent spirit.

"Isn't it a dandy, Jim? I hunted all over town to find it. You'll have to look at the time a hundred times a day now. Give me your watch. I want to see how it looks on it."

Instead of obeying, Jim tumbled down on the couch and put his hands under the back of his head and smiled.

"Dell," said he, "let's put our Christmas presents away and keep 'em a while. They're too nice to use just at present. I sold the watch to get the money to buy your combs. And now suppose you put the chops on."

-- he Gift of the Magi, O. Henry (1917)

*I*t was nearly midnight by the time Dare made it back to the palace. His mission had been more successful than he could have dreamed. He raced up the stairs to Lyric, wanting nothing more than to share her joy at finally regaining her sight. She must have used the Wish by now.

Or perhaps she was waiting for him, so he could be there when she did. He hoped that she had. And when she saw...

Almost before he knocked, she threw open the door and launched herself into his arms. He barely had time to put the long, thin package down on the floor before he caught her.

He whirled her around, kissing and kissing her, and kicked the door shut behind them. When he finally managed to let her go, she was laughing and breathless.

"Lyric. Tell me. Did you use it? The Wish? Can you see?"

She took a deep breath. "I did use the Wish, but not for my sight. Let me show you."

She moved as quickly as caution allowed to the bed and drew a small wrapped object from beneath her pillow. "This is it, my darling. Isn't it wonderful? I think you'll be the happiest captain on the high seas now, my love."

She put the package in his hand and waited, beaming, as he slowly unwrapped it. Even before the wrapping fell away, though, he knew. He could feel it; could sense his bond with Seranth returning.

"Oh, Lyric. Oh, my love. *Mi amara.*" He didn't understand why his eyes were burning. Why he couldn't swallow past the lump that was suddenly in his throat. " I could never, ever deserve you, not if I worked at it for a thousand years, but you can believe that I will spend every minute of that time trying."

He put the band down on the table and pulled her back into his arms. Never, ever, in the more than a century of his existence, had anyone made a sacrifice for him. And *this*? To sacrifice the possibility of regaining her sight? A fierce wave of emotion caught in his throat until he couldn't talk and wasn't sure he could breathe.

"*Mi amara*—my beloved. Will you marry me and give me many beautiful babies who look just like their mother?"

"Yes. Yes, a thousand times yes." She put her arms around his neck, and when he bent his head to hers, her eyes were shining. "Dare, I know it's late, but can't we go out to your ship now so I can meet Seranth? I've been so excited to see your ship and meet her. Let's do it. It will be part of our Christmas miracle."

He smiled at her, but gently shook his head. "Let's go downstairs and meet everyone for the Christmas Eve feast instead. We'll have plenty of time to look at our presents."

"But—"

He took her hands and kissed them, one by one. "Tomorrow we'll find the perfect stone for your ring. But tonight, let's feast."

"But--"

He smiled at her but knew she couldn't see it, so he placed her hands on the sides of his face. " Lyric, I sold my ship to buy you a lost Renoir. I wanted the first thing you saw with your new eyes to be an object of ultimate beauty."

At that, she started to cry. "But your ship—"

"Don't you understand by now?" He tightened his arms around her and put his heart into her hands, knowing that she would protect it. Knowing that his future belonged to her, and hers to him. "All I will ever need is you, my very own Christmas miracle. Anything else is just a bonus. Let's go down to that feast. Maybe we can make Alaric sing Christmas carols."

And so with laughter—and a few more tears—Dare and Lyric went down to join the rest of their Atlantean family for a Christmas supper, and to share their wonderful news.

15

The magi, as you know, were wise men—wonderfully wise men—who brought gifts to the Babe in the manger. They invented the art of giving Christmas presents. Being wise, their gifts were no doubt wise ones, possibly bearing the privilege of exchange in case of duplication. And here I have lamely related to you the uneventful chronicle of two foolish children in a flat who most unwisely sacrificed for each other the greatest treasures of their house. But in a last word to the wise of these days let it be said that of all who give gifts these two were the wisest. O all who give and receive gifts, such as they are wisest. Everywhere they are wisest. They are the magi.

-- The Gift of the Magi, O. Henry (1917)

*C*hristmas morning in Atlantis.

Lyric almost pinched herself again, but this time the very large, very muscular man in her bed did it for her.

"Hey!"

He sighed. "I know. I'm sorry. I just can't keep my hands

off that lovely round ass of yours. I may never accomplish anything again for dreaming about it."

"That is the strangest compliment anybody has ever given me." She put her arms around his neck and pulled him to her for a kiss. "Merry Christmas."

"Merry Christmas," he said, before rolling on top of her and pinning her arms over her head with one hand. "Time for your present."

He moved his body against her in a determined fashion, and she had to laugh. "I think you already gave me that present."

"Then you should return it to me," he told her solemnly. "It's the gift that keeps on giving."

So she did.

And it was quite a while before they lay back on the bed, gasping.

"You love me," the pirate in her bed—in her heart—said smugly, all arrogance and charm.

"I do," she admitted. "Just let me catch my breath, and I'll show you how much again."

He rolled over to face her. "Lyric," he said, and his voice was unexpectedly serious. "I can't—I can never—"

"Dare," she said, putting her entire heart in her voice, so he was sure to hear it. "All I need to see is you."

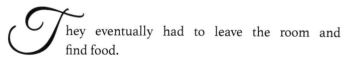

*T*hey eventually had to leave the room and find food.

"Or I'll collapse right here on the floor," Lyric laughingly told him when they finally made it out of the shower, boneless with aftershock and satisfaction.

His stomach growled, right on cue. "I think you might be right."

When they walked into the dining hall, hand in hand, a crowd of children, all of whom had been impressed by Lyric's beautiful singing voice, crowded around and demanded a story and a song.

Lyric smiled at their clamoring. "A story, too?"

"Yes, yes," they all chorused. "An Earth Christmas story from Topside."

She sank down on the cushion they'd saved for her, but never let go of Dare's hand, so he dropped down to the cushion next to hers. "This is my favorite Christmas story of all, so gather around and listen closely. It's a story of love and hope and the miracle of Christmas."

When they were all settled, their little rapt faces staring up at her, Dare thought his heart might have grown too large for his chest, because he was having a hard time breathing while looking at this amazing woman who had become the center of his life.

"I love you," he told her, not caring who heard him.

The children all started giggling.

"I love you, too," she said. And then she smiled at him, with infinite love and joy and hope shining in her face, and began.

"One dollar and eighty-seven cents..."

EPILOGUE

One year later...

One year later...
Lyric placed her hand on the slight round-ness of her belly and smiled. The sea spirit, hovering in place next to her at the bow of the ship, was singing a song in a language even Dare hadn't recognized. It was older than any known civilization, Seranth had informed them in a wistful voice.

It had taken no more than the space of an instant for Lyric to love the water elemental as much as Dare did, when they'd finally been able to buy the *Luna* back from its new owner. Dare had captained a merchant ship for a while, and she'd painted furiously to populate a show at an Atlantean gallery. Her "rare, *human* paintings of the world Above," as the canny gallery owner had labeled them, had sold like hotcakes to the Atlanteans who'd never yet ventured out of Atlantis.

And now they were finally back on the ship Dare loved, making perfectly legitimate supply runs and carrying perfectly legitimate cargo—and the occasional visiting dignitary—to and from Atlantis.

Seranth, who felt like the sister Lyric had always wanted, hummed while she petted Picasso, who was purring loudly in her arms. "We're going to have a baby on this ship, are we not?"

Lyric nodded. "We are. But Seranth, please don't tell Dare yet. I want to surprise him."

A thudding noise behind her signaled that her wicked pirate had finished fixing the lines and dropped back onto the deck. He strode over to her and pulled her back against him, resting his chin on the top of her head.

"Surprise me with what?"

"I'll be up in the crow's nest," Seranth said, releasing Picasso to scamper off and sun himself.

Lyric turned in his arms and held her face up for his kiss. "I love you, you know, my wicked pirate."

"The Painter and the Wicked Pirate. Is Meredith really still planning to write that novel?"

She laughed. "Planning to? She's already written and published it. I bet it will be a bestseller. I need to call her and suggest the title for the sequel."

He tightened his arms around her and kissed her; long, slow, sensuous kisses that promised an evening of deliciously wicked seduction.

"So what is it?" he asked, when he raised his head.

She blinked, still dazed from his kisses. "What is what?"

"The title of the next romance novel. What is it?"

She felt the smile spread across her face. "The Painter and the Wicked Pirate's Baby."

There was a pause, and then his hand slid down to her belly. "Oh, my love. How is it possible to be so completely and entirely happy, and then find that your heart can contain even more joy?"

"It's the miracle of Christmas," she said.

Dare's arms tightened around her. "It's a good damn day to be a pirate."

And the painter and her pirate lived happily—and wickedly—ever after.

~

*N*OTE FROM ALYSSA DAY:
     I have to get a little sentimental here and tell you how much I appreciate you for reading Christmas in Atlantis. *This job is a dream come true, and I wouldn't have it except for readers like you. I adored writing this book—I've had the idea in mind for a long time.* The Gift of the Magi *is one of my favorite stories in the world, and I wanted to pay homage to it in a way that did it justice, especially on this centennial anniversary of its publication.*

I'm thrilled to announce that Poseidon's Warriors will continue with A Year of Atlantis in 2018—a book per month— and you'll find out how Atlantis's independent, brave, strong warriors will cope with their matchmaking queen, who is determined to find them all true love. The next book is January in Atlantis, *and it's available for preorder now at select retailers and will be available to all on release day: January 16, 2018.*

If you want the scoop on all new releases, behind-the-scenes details, and the chance to win prizes, **Text ALYSSADAY to 66866** *to sign up for my newsletter. I promise never to sell, fold, spindle, or mutilate your information so you will get no spam—ever —from me.*

You can also follow me on BookBub *if you only want new release news.*

Thanks again for reading—you rock!
Alyssa

THANK YOU!

Thanks so much for reading *Christmas in Atlantis*. I hope you had as much fun reading it as I did writing it.

Want the scoop about new books? Text ALYSSADAY to 66866! Find out when my next book is available, get special bonus-only-for-subscribers, behind-the-scenes info, and win cool stuff! (No spam, because I would NEVER sell my mailing list!) And/or follow me on twitter at @alyssa_day, Instagram at @authoralyssaday, or like my Facebook page at http://facebook.com/authoralyssaday.

Review it. My family hides the chocolate if I don't mention that reviews help other readers find new books, so if you have the time, please consider leaving one. I appreciate all reviews, and thank you for your time.

Try my other books! You can find excerpts of all of my books at http://alyssaday.com. Read on for an excerpt from the first in my new sexy and funny Cardinal Witches series, **Alejandro's Sorceress.**

HALLOWEEN IN ATLANTIS

The Warrior's Creed:

We will wait. And watch. And protect.
And serve as first warning on the eve of humanity's destruction.
Then, and only then, Atlantis will rise.
For we are the Warriors of Poseidon, and the mark of the Trident
we bear serves as witness to our sacred duty to safeguard
mankind.

CHAPTER 1

A *tlantis*

*L*IAM pointed his dagger at the glowing orange object that stared menacingly up at him, its teeth bared in a snarl. "Stand back, Eric. I'll kill it. Considering the unbelievable mutants that swarmed here during the demon infestation, we have no idea what this might be."

The small boy following him edged back and away from the rocks that formed a barrier between the wild grasses and the pounding surf. "Is it a demon, Liam? Are we in danger? Should I go protect the little prince?"

Liam's lips quirked up in a smile that he quickly suppressed. The youngling hadn't reached his tenth birthday, and yet his first thought was to protect others. It wouldn't do to let him think Liam was mocking him.

"I don't think it's a demon, but better to take no chances,

in case it's unfriendly magic. It might be a spell-trap, or an evil charm, or--"

"A fruit. It's actually just a fruit," said a decidedly feminine and somewhat exasperated-sounding voice. "And if you kill my jack-o'-lantern, I might have to hurt you."

It was her. Of *course* it was her. Liam couldn't believe he hadn't felt her approach in his nerve endings, or just beneath his skin, where she seemed most often to lodge.

He sheathed the dagger, took a deep breath, and turned to face the most annoying, irritating, and, if he were honest with himself—and he always tried to be, in spite of his family—the most *intriguing* human he'd ever met.

It didn't help that she was so beautiful. Or that the purple dress she wore wrapped around her curvy body like a lover's caress.

"Why is your fruit glowing?" he demanded, and immediately felt like a fool. Behind him, Eric snickered.

"It's a pumpkin," Jaime said in a long-suffering voice, her fascinating chocolate brown eyes sparkling with what was no doubt amusement at his expense. "A jack-o'-lantern. A simple and traditional Halloween decoration. We carve interesting things into them and then put candles inside, so they glow and look pretty for Halloween parties."

She was explaining the fruit, and he knew he should listen, but she was just so damn easy to look at. Silky dark hair, the ends tipped with an unnatural but enticing purple, fell in careless waves around her face. Those amazing eyes, set in an arresting face that was all honey-golden skin and kissable red lips.

Kissable?

He scrubbed a hand over his face. He needed to head for the training grounds and go a few rounds with one of Poseidon's new warrior trainees. An hour or two of hard exertion might clear his brain, which had seemed to malfunction whenever he'd been around this woman during the month she'd been on Atlantis.

He looked at her again. That luscious body with curves a man could hold on to while he . . .

Maybe he'd need *three* hours at the training grounds.

He shook his head to clear it. What he'd seen as a potential threat wasn't a demon at all. It was a, what did she call it? A jack-o'-lantern. Liam felt like a fool.

The feeling wasn't new, which made it all the more grating.

"Inviting humans to Atlantis in such high numbers was a mistake," he said, putting ice in his tone. "It is nearly impossible to maintain the proper security for the royal family, when hordes of unknown people and their--"

"Fruit?" She smiled sweetly and then pretended to cringe. "Oh, no, protect me, Liam! A flying banana is heading my way!"

Everything in him stilled. She was . . . she was *teasing* him. He, the son and heir to the worst bunch of petty criminals that Atlantis had probably ever known—the one man from whom mothers had always hidden their daughters. Now that he was grown, even as one of Poseidon's warriors and King Conlan's elite guard, Atlantean women treated him like the low-born trash his family had always been. Almost always, if what Keely had told him about a long-dead high priest, Nereus, being his ancestor. But this woman —this beautiful, maddening human—was teasing him, and her eyes were sparkling up at him with amusement, not malice.

Liam had learned the difference between the two very well over the course of a lifetime lived in the shadow of his family's misdeeds.

She was teasing him, and he was in a great deal of trouble, because he wanted to beg her not to stop. He took a step closer, almost involuntarily drawn to her, and her eyes widened. He glanced down at her parted lips and had to force himself not to dip his head and taste them.

"If you like fruit, I can introduce you to Atlantean blushberries," he murmured, for her ears only, although he could see that Eric had become bored and was wading in the surf a dozen paces away. "I've heard that they have certain aphrodisiacal properties, when consumed with the right wine."

Jaime's breath seemed to stutter as she looked up at him; both of them frozen in the moment. She put a hand up as if to touch his chest, but then hastily shoved it in the pocket of her pants. "As if you'd need aphrodisiacs, looking like *that*," she muttered.

He started laughing before he even realized he was doing it. "So you like how I look? I can assure you, the feeling is mutual."

She backed up a pace, shaking her head. Her hair swept her shoulders in a flurry of chestnut and purple waves that he wanted to touch. Wanted to see spread over his pillows.

Jaime raised a hand to her mouth. He was suddenly struck by a twinge of jealousy that it was her fingers touching her lips, not his, and he realized he was quite possibly losing his mind right here in front of the fruit. He had enough problems trying to overcome his family's legacy and prove himself. The *last* thing he needed was to fall in love.

"Your eyes are glowing, Liam," she whispered. "That can't be good."

CHAPTER 2

Jaime Radcliffe took a deep breath of the crisp, salty ocean air and suddenly realized that she might be in actual danger. She'd deliberately teased this man —this *Atlantean warrior*—with no thought of consequences or repercussions. She'd only been in Atlantis for six weeks; in fact, the entire world had only known Atlantis even existed for not much longer than that. She'd been excited and honored to have been chosen as the queen's first party planner, and she'd been unbelievably thrilled to get the chance to see this land that had risen from deep beneath the ocean and straight out of legend into the world landscape. Walking around the palace grounds and staring at ancient, delicate and graceful marble spires on buildings that looked like they belonged on a movie set had been an amazing adventure.

Not to mention, it had been a great time to get out of town and away from yet another in a long string of disappointing boyfriends. This one had decided, after only three months of dating, that it might be a good idea for him to quit his job and become her "partner" in the business.

Her partner. In a business she'd spent five years building.

Her exact words had been "not in this lifetime," and that had been the end of him. She hadn't missed him at all, which told her an uncomfortable amount about how much she'd cared about him in the first place. No matter. He was history, and she was currently living in a place that was *real* history and myth all rolled up into one beautiful, unbelievable package: Atlantis. The lost continent. City of dreams, long thought to have been nothing more than a teaching example made up by Plato on a particularly imaginative day.

But it was real. And so was Liam. And reading the Atlantis informational packet, with its overview of Atlantean laws and traditions, had done nothing to prepare her for an up-close and personal confrontation with this man. Maybe teasing one of Poseidon's warriors was a hanging offense, or she'd be forced to walk the plank at sundown. Not that this was a ship, but, wow, the man was frying her brain cells.

This *man*. He was unlike anyone she'd ever met before. Sure, he had the typical Atlantean tall, dark, and gorgeous thing going on, but Liam was ... different. Something about him had caught her attention from the first moment she'd laid eyes on him. Queen Riley had called him over to introduce them, and he'd stalked toward them from across the garden, all grace and power and pure, primal male. Jaime's mouth had dried out, and she'd almost tripped over her own tongue, just trying to say hello. And, if she hadn't been mistaken, there'd been a gleam of amusement or maybe sympathy in the queen's eyes after Liam had gone.

Riley had smiled. "I had the same reaction to Conlan when I met him. They can be somewhat overwhelming, can't they?"

Jaime had nodded, remembering a snippet of fact from somewhere that the queen had been—still was? —human. "He's certainly that," she'd agreed, staring at Liam's delectable backside as he'd walked away. "Oh, boy."

And now, the man's eyes were glowing. Glowing. Deep, ocean-drowning blue, touched with liquid silver, as if his eyes were lit up from within like one of her jack-o'-lanterns. He was well over six feet of thickly muscled, deadly warrior, and his eyes were glowing with heat and danger. She should be scared to death.

Instead, she wanted to climb him like a tree and lick the side of his neck. Well, sure, he was spectacularly gorgeous, like every other Atlantean warrior she'd met, but there was just something *more* when she looked at him. Black, silky hair fell in waves to his collar, framing a fallen-angel face that must cause every woman on the formerly lost continent to fantasize about him. That warrior body, with broad shoulders tapering down to narrow hips and powerful legs, currently encased in dark pants, a carelessly tucked-in white long-sleeved shirt with the sleeves rolled up, and leather boots, was enough to make any woman take a second look.

And a third, and a fourth . . .

It was the humor in his eyes that had caught her, though. That, and the kindness. That was all Liam, and it was perhaps what made it so hard for her to ignore him. But he was Danger with a capital D, not at all the type of man she usually went for. Her type was sweet and funny and nice.

And lets you boss him around.

No, that couldn't be true. She wasn't bossy. She was an event organizer. It was her career. She had to be *organized*.

So, she made lists. Lots and lots and lots of lists. Better to make lists and get things done than be the kind of person who falls into bed with the first Atlantean warrior who made her nipples tingle just by looking at her with his glowing eyes.

"Oh, boy," she said, sighing and trying to think of anything else but tingling. "You, um, I—I'm sorry I teased you. I don't really want to walk the plank."

He tilted his head, but at least the glow in his eyes was fading, and she was almost positive he was fighting a smile. "What in the nine hells are you talking about?"

Even his voice was sexy, and all the rest of the parts of her that hadn't tingled in a very long time woke up and noticed. Which was bad. Very bad.

"You have nine hells? We only have one. Um, never mind. The party is starting in only a few hours, and I have to finish placing the jack-o'-lanterns," she babbled, wondering what had happened to calm, organized, Jaime, the most unflappable event organizer in Chicago. This was her, being flappable. Very flappable. Flapped, even.

She groaned.

"I can't do you right now. Do *this!* I can't do this," she said, feeling her face catch on fire.

He leaned closer, and all the oxygen in the world disappeared. "Oh, you sweet, sexy human. I promise that I am looking forward to the time when you *can* do me, as you put it."

"Pumpkins," she blurted out, when it looked like he was going to kiss her. "I need to get these pumpkins unloaded."

"Pumpkins?"

She pointed to a motorized cart, like a golf cart but with a bed in the back like a pickup truck. "Pumpkins. I have to go. Put jack-o'-lanterns all over the place. For the party."

She closed her eyes and took a deep breath. Focus. She

needed to quit lusting over the hot Atlantean and get on with things.

But then she felt his arms go around her waist and her brain short-circuited. Her eyes flew open and he was right there. In front of her. Staring down at her, laughter and something else in his expression.

Heat. The heat of a man who wanted her, and this had nothing to do with magic or glowing or anything else. This was wanting, pure and simple, and it tugged at her until she wanted to wrap herself around his body and cling to him.

Naked.

"I need to distribute the pumpkins," she said instead, practically hyperventilating. This was why she'd tried to hide every time she'd seen him around since she'd been on Atlantis. Somehow, she'd known he'd be dangerous to her.

"Fruit again. You're obsessed with fruit, I think," he said, not bothering to hide the slow, predatory smile that spread across his incredible face. "I'd rather you were obsessed with me."

"I need--"

He cut her off, his eyes filled with what looked like bewilderment. "I need, too. I don't understand it, but you make me need. And want. Things that probably aren't good for me; things that I can never have. I don't even know you yet, but you make me want."

The stark confession tore at something inside her. Looking into his eyes, she almost thought she could glimpse an aching void of loneliness, just for an instant.

"You make me want, too," she admitted. It was a moment out of time; a moment that needed honesty.

A flash of purely masculine triumph crossed his face, and then he bent his head to hers. "Then let us taste what is between us, just for a moment."

Her laugh was shaky. "Yeah, okay. Maybe we can get it out of our systems."

His smile faded. "I don't think so."

And then he took her mouth, and gravity stopped working.

Electricity sparked between them, inside her, around her. The heat of his big, hard body against hers, the touch of his skin, the taste of his mouth—it all overwhelmed her with sensation. Someone was moaning, and she thought it might be her, but she didn't even care; she clutched at his shoulders, trying to get closer, needing to get closer, to climb inside him and curl up, wrapped in the sensual heat of his kiss.

Liam's hands were suddenly on her butt, pulling her even closer, and she twined her hands into his hair, touching his head, his face, his neck, while he kissed her in a way she'd never been kissed before.

Heat seared through her; heat and need, heat and want. She moaned again, against his lips, and he made a low, growling sound that shuddered through her body like an earthquake.

He finally raised his head and stared down at her, and both of them were breathing hard, like they'd been running. It occurred to Jaime that it was exactly what she *should* be doing. Running. As fast and as far as she could, to get away from this man who had sliced through her defenses like a sword through a pumpkin.

Laughter bubbled out of her. "Oh, wow, that's it. You're a fruit ninja."

CHAPTER 3

Liam's sense exploded with the feel of the delightfully unpredictable woman in his arms, and with the spicy, flowery scent of her hair and skin. He wanted nothing more than to carry her off to a private place and touch and taste every inch of her wonderfully sexy body.

"Yuck!"

Liam glanced over his shoulder and saw Eric running back toward the palace, probably disgusted with tagging along behind a warrior uncle who wasn't behaving in a very warrior-like manner. He grinned ruefully but let his nephew go. The boy was probably meant to be home doing chores, anyway.

Or learning how to pick pockets, knowing Liam's brother.

"Liam?" She was looking at him with her beautiful brown eyes, and—this close to her--he could see fascinating flecks of gold in them.

She probably wanted him to talk. Women usually did. He only wanted to kiss her again, but she seemed to expect some response to her confusing comment about the fruit ninjas.

"I am one of Poseidon's warriors, not a ninja. We have encountered ninjas, and they are usually much shorter than me."

She laughed even harder.

"Why is that funny?"

She started to respond, but then glanced at the silver watch on her wrist and gasped. "Oh, no! Liam, I am completely off schedule. Please, you have to let me go. I can't mess this up. There are more than a thousand people showing up for this party, and it has to go perfectly for the queen. My professional reputation is on the line and, more than that, I really like her."

She bit her lip, and he immediately released her. He realized he'd do anything to erase the look of distress on her face. Slay vampires. Fight demons.

Carry pumpkins.

He sighed. "What can I do to help?"

"Really?" She flashed a smile over her shoulder as she rushed over to the cart. "That would be amazing. I just need to drop these off, make a last-minute check with the caterer, and then get into costume and be ready to unobtrusively make this party be a smash."

Liam didn't even try not to look at her lusciously round ass when she bent over the side of the cart to get another of the jack-o'-lanterns, and he wasn't embarrassed when she caught him doing it.

"It's a truly world-class ass," he said honestly, delighted to see her blush.

Thirty minutes and twice as many pumpkins later, they were down to five more fruit to distribute. Jaime had the perfect place for each jack-o'-lantern on her list, which was frustrating enough, since he'd planned on just dumping them wherever so they could get back to the kissing. However, there was also the time needed to turn on the small, battery-powered lights inside each one.

"You know, we could have asked someone to light these up magically," he pointed out, lifting out one of the biggest pumpkins for the gazebo nearest Poseidon's fountain.

Jaime brushed her hair out of her face and glanced up at him, lifting her own pumpkin into her arms. "Really? Can you do that?"

He laughed. "No, not me. That's not my magic. I could have made you forget you needed to do anything with pumpkins, ever again, though, and right about now I'm regretting that I didn't."

"You can do that? Mess with somebody's memory?" Her eyes widened, and he silently cursed his stupidity. The last thing he'd wanted to do was scare her.

"Only when I must, and—wait. Why is this pumpkin rattling? I think your light must be broken inside or something, Jaime." He put the fruit down on the edge of the cart and reached for the stem of the carefully carved-out top, which was much wider than the others had been, for some reason.

When he looked into the pumpkin, he hurled the top to the ground and let loose with a sizzling stream of virulently strong curses in ancient Atlantean, as disbelief and then rage tore through him.

He looked up to see Jaime staring at him, her face turning paler by the second. "Liam, what's wrong? I'm a party planner, and even I wouldn't react that strongly to a broken light in a decoration."

He reached into the pumpkin and carefully withdrew the object that had been rattling against the unbroken light.

Rays from the afternoon sun slanted down on it, almost as if to highlight the delicate beauty of the thing that in no possible world should have been inside a pumpkin on the bottom of a pile in a cart.

Jaime gasped. "Is that--"

"Queen Riley's crown," Liam said grimly. "Somebody is in for a world of pain."

Jaime shook her head, looking totally bewildered. "I don't understand. Why is her crown inside a pumpkin? Is it some weird Atlantis tradition, no offense, that you guys hide the royal jewels on Halloween?"

The idea of it momentarily distracted him. "Weird Atlantis tradition? This from the woman carving fruit and dressing people up in costumes that are meant to be frightening? Like vampires and monsters?"

"Don't forget clowns," she added. "But, point taken. So I guess this shouldn't be here. Why--" Her mouth rounded in an O of comprehension. "You think somebody was stealing it? Hiding it in the pumpkin for later?"

"That is exactly what I think, and now we find out who, and this will be the last Halloween they will ever encounter," Liam replied.

"You don't—you don't think I had anything to do with this, do you?" Jaime's hand crept up to her throat. "I swear to you that I'd never--"

"Never have asked me to help with the pumpkins that contained the missing crown?" He shook his head. "Not to mention, Queen Riley is an empath. She'd never have trusted you if you were deceitful or a thief. Believe me."

He had first-hand knowledge of that. The one time the queen had met his brother had not gone well. He was thankful that neither Riley nor Conlan were the type to judge a man for his family's crimes.

"Okay. Thank you." Jaime glanced at the crown, and then at her watch again, clearly torn. "I want to help, but I still need to finish everything on my list. Unless you're canceling the party over this? Please, please tell me you're not canceling the party."

Liam wanted to cancel it. He suddenly fiercely wanted to evict every non-Atlantean except Jaime and never let them back in. How one of them had dared to steal the queen's crown, he had no idea, but he planned to find out.

Unless it's not one of the outsiders at all, his conscience sneered at him. *It's probably one of your family members.*

No. *Hells,* no.

If it *had* been any of his family, he'd kill them himself, and damn the consequences.

"No. King Conlan wouldn't want us to cancel the queen's party over this. In fact, he probably wouldn't want her to know about it at all. So keep quiet, okay? Go and do what you need to do, but not a word about any of this."

She nodded, but still looked worried. "Of course. Not a word."

He carefully put the crown inside his shirt and left the pumpkin on the edge of the fountain. "I don't want to be seen carrying this, in case the culprit or culprits see me, but I need it to be readily available in case Alaric wants to scan it for magical resonance."

If any of them could play magical detective quickly and easily, it would be the most powerful high priest Atlantis had even known.

Jaime nodded and then took a hesitant step toward him and put her hand on his arm. "Liam. I just—be careful."

Warmth swept through him like a wave breaking against one of Atlantis's many beaches. This human female—this charming, bewildering, beautiful human female—was worried about him. He couldn't find the words to respond, but he gently took her face in his hands and kissed her again. Just a brief pressure of lips; a reassurance and a promise.

"I'll see you when this is resolved, and we will finish our earlier conversation," he said, and was rewarded with the hot pink blush that spread over her lovely curved cheeks.

"Caterer," she blurted out, and then she turned and walked away so fast she was practically running.

"Thieves," he said, and headed for the palace. Someone was about to be very, very sorry.

tlantis, the throne room

Liam nodded to the guard at the door and strode into the throne room, wondering why the king's brother, Ven, would be there. Ven, known to friends as a jokester and connoisseur of B monster films, but to enemies as the King's Vengeance, was lounging on the steps at the base of the throne he'd sworn he'd never take. Nobody had been happier than Ven when Conlan and Riley's son Aidan was born; he wasn't the marble columns and gold throne type.

Ven looked up and grinned. "Hey, Liam, what's up? Hiding from the party, too?"

A second man, one Liam hadn't seen in a while, leaned against a wall and nodded a hello. Denal, one of Conlan's elite Seven, had come back from wherever he'd been on mission this time. The usually cheerful warrior had new lines on his face and a hardness to his eyes that Liam recognized very well. He saw it reflected back at him whenever he looked in a mirror. Like Denal, he had seen and done some very bad things, all in the name of fighting the evil that lurked in the dark corners of the world.

All of them had. For the past eleven thousand years, the sea god himself had tasked generations upon generations of his sworn warriors to protect humanity from the monsters that preyed upon them. Even when the portal had been their only way to get to the surface, they'd carried out the mission. Now, when the world was open to all of them, all the time, they were trying to renegotiate their understanding of Atlantis's place in the world.

"Hiding, no, Your Highness," Liam told Ven. "But somebody has been doing some hiding."

Ven rolled his eyes. "Call me Your Highness again, and I'll kick your ass."

Denal snickered, his grim darkness lightening for a moment. "Whatever you say, Your Majesty."

Liam didn't know whether to laugh or duck. He hadn't spent nearly as much time with either of them as they had with each other, and this had the feeling of a well-worn routine. But he had more important business to discuss than royal titles.

"I'm sorry to report that we have one or more thieves at hand today," Liam informed them.

"Other than your brother?" Ven's tone was wry, but Liam could feel the burn of shame crawling up his neck.

"I told him to stay home." Liam pulled the crown out of his shirt and held it up. "Look what I found. In a fruit."

"Riley's crown? Where did you get this?" Ven stood up and took the crown and then sniffed it. "And what in the nine hells is that smell?"

"Pumpkin guts," Liam said. "Jaime Radcliffe and I--"

Ven raised an eyebrow. "Jaime, huh? I've noticed you mooning over the party planner since she got here."

Liam forced his expression to blankness. "I have no idea what you're talking about. Do you want to hear about the queen's crown, or should we talk about our feelings and braid each other's hair?"

Ven laughed and made a go-ahead motion with the hand not holding the crown.

Liam explained what he and Jaime had found. "Somebody was planning to come back for that pumpkin."

Denal straightened from where he'd been leaning against the wall and pinned Liam with a hard stare. "Yeah. Sounds like an inside job. Maybe somebody who knew the party girl would discover the crown, so he had to pretend to find it first. Maybe somebody who grew up learning how to be a thief over his breakfast eggs."

Rage smashed through Liam's self-control like a battering ram, and his fingers automatically twitched toward his dagger.

"Don't even think about it," Ven advised in a drawl. "And Denal, shut the hell up. Conlan wouldn't have named Liam to the Warriors if there was the slightest shred of doubt about his character."

The temperature in the room instantly dropped about ten degrees, and all three of them swung around to the doorway, knowing who it must be before he even appeared.

"High Priest Alaric," Liam said, bowing.

"He's retired from the priest business," said the small, dark-haired woman who walked in the room with Alaric-- his wife, Quinn. She was also retired, from being the co-leader of the North American rebels. Liam spared a thought to wonder which one of them was the more intimidating to outsiders.

"He's scarier," Quinn said, as if she'd read his mind. But

he knew her gift was that she was an *aknasha*, an emotional empath, not a mind reader.

Alaric raised a brow, and Quinn smiled at him. "I'm the funny one."

"Flirt with the warrior at his own risk, my love," Alaric said, in a voice so full of thunder and darkness that Liam was surprised the walls didn't shake.

"Isn't that supposed to be 'at *your* own risk,'?" she asked her husband.

"You know I won't hurt *you*," Alaric responded, baring his teeth in a feral smile. "Him, I'll kill."

"I would prefer not to die until after I solve this mystery and capture the thief or thieves, my lord," Liam said.

"Unless he stole it himself," Denal growled.

Quinn walked up to Liam and stared into his eyes, which made him slightly concerned that Alaric would strike him dead with a magical bolt of lightning at any second.

"Nope," she said. "He didn't do it. He's pissed off and determined to find who did this. He's also . . . um, never mind."

She winked at him, and he suddenly had the gut-level certainty that she was reading his feelings for Jaime. Damn empaths.

Ven grinned. "Also what? Riled up after hanging out with Jaime?"

"None of your business, brother-in-law of mine," Quinn said. "Now, does Riley know about this? Did they steal anything else? Do we have any idea who did it?"

"As usual, your wife cuts through the clutter to get right to the point," Ven told Alaric.

"I was hoping one of you could determine whether or not more of the queen's jewels have been taken," Liam said.

"Jaime--Ms. Radcliffe--hopes that you will not cancel the party."

Quinn whistled. "Oh, no. We definitely can't cancel the party over this, or Riley will kill us all. She's gone all in on this shindig."

Alaric frowned. "I would be happy to call this nonsense off."

Quinn poked her husband in the side, to Liam's amazement. Even a few short years ago, the idea that anyone in the former high priest's five-hundred-year-long life would dare to poke him, let alone get close enough even to touch him, would never have occurred to anyone on the Seven Isles. But now the powerful Alaric stared at Quinn with fierce possessiveness that made Liam ache to feel that much for a woman.

Jaime's face, her lips swollen from his kisses, popped into his mind, and Quinn coughed. Liam's face burned, knowing she could feel his emotions with her high-level empath nature.

"Your pardon, my lady, but I would prefer if you stay out of my emotions."

Quinn smiled ruefully. "I'd prefer it, too, but I'm stuck with it. So quit *feeling* so much. Just go get her, McHottie."

Alaric growled and his eyes started to glow hot green. Liam took another step away from Quinn, just in case.

"Oh, relax. It's what Keely called him, remember?" Quinn said, grinning. "Hey, I don't mean to be overly casual about this, but is there any chance this is a prank? And speaking of Keely, she's an object reader. If only she and Justice were here, she could tell us who had the crown last."

"Justice and Liam in the same room might not be a great idea, given the McHottie thing and Justice's psycho jealousy,

Sis," Ven said, grinning. "Unless we want to pick pieces of Liam up off the walls."

"I can hold my own," Liam said calmly, but the bantering was beginning to get on his nerves. He'd always been a loner and was still unused to the back and forth that clearly was the norm with Conlan, Alaric, and the Seven. "And who would attempt such a thing as a prank? The new queen's coronation crown is far too important for that."

Just then, Jaime ran into the room, and Liam automatically started toward her, with some vague notion of protecting her. When she ran straight to him, something that had been tightly clenched inside him eased.

She took a second to catch her breath, then shook her head. "I don't think it's a prank. My caterer is missing. Not to be melodramatic, but I kind of suspect foul play. And it gets worse."

CHAPTER 5

J aime froze, suddenly realizing that she was in the formal throne room, where she'd never spent any time—and didn't know if outsiders were even allowed in-- surrounded by four of Atlantis's most dangerous warriors. And one of them was the former high priest that everybody had warned her about. Apparently he ate small children for fun, or something. On second thought, considering the way he was glaring at everybody in the room who wasn't his wife (and *she* was the queen's sister —yikes!), maybe he *did* eat small children—or at least troublesome party planners.

"How much worse?" Liam asked, looking grim.

"The boats are early. The partygoers are here, now."

"Send them away," Alaric commanded, and Jaime flinched, expecting to be smote any second. Or was it smitten? No, that was what she was with Liam.

Ack! No. Wait.

Smited. She was almost sure it was smited. Not that it mattered, and why was she doing the mental-ramble polka?

Her brain was like a hamster on a wheel—on crack. A crack hamster. Yep. That's it.

She was totally losing it.

Alaric scowled at her when she didn't immediately answer, and Liam moved so that he was standing between her and the priest. Jaime blew out a sigh of relief at first. And then she got mad at herself for being a chicken, defiantly sidestepped Liam's attempt to stop her, and walked out into the middle of the room.

"Look. You're all scary and everything, but we have jewel thiefs—um, jewel *thieves*—and missing caterers to deal with, not to mention the biggest party of my career. So are any of you going to help me, or are you going to keep standing around looking mean and intimidating?" She ran out of air and sucked in a deep breath before noticing that one of the guys she'd just called mean and intimidating was the king's brother.

Great.

Why not insult the *entire* royal family while she was at it? It's not like she wanted to work ever again. She could just sit around, eat bon bons, and watch her career flush down a giant Atlantean toilet.

Ven laughed, though, instead of yelling "off with her head," and everybody else at least smiled. Even Alaric. Well, the corner of his lips moved a fraction of an inch, but that might be as close as he got to smiling.

In spite of her earlier boldness, she found herself edging closer to Liam. He was openly grinning at her, as if she were a child who'd done something especially clever.

And Quinn? She laughed out loud. "Oh, I'm going to like you a lot, Jaime. You've got to have balls or brains to stand up to this lot, and it looks like you've got both. Figuratively speaking. And we're definitely going to help."

Alaric groaned, his eyes flashing a hot silvery color, and Quinn put her hands on her hips. "Look, buddy, this has nothing to do with Yetis or basilisks, so you can just suck it up and help."

The other warrior in the room—Denal—laughed at that, and Alaric narrowed his eyes and casually waved a hand. A streak of blue energy shot from the ex-priest's hand toward Denal and lifted him into the air until he was floating just beneath the chandelier twenty feet above.

"Not funny," Denal shouted, and this time Ven and Liam both laughed.

Quinn rolled her eyes, but then turned to Jaime, and this time she was all business. "What happened? We know about the pumpkins and the crown."

"I went to talk to my caterer about any last minute preparations, problems, or persnicketies—that's what I call it, the three Ps—and he was gone. Worse, he has apparently been gone for more than an hour, but nobody called me," Jaime explained, her voice rising to just short of hysterical. "I've worked with him for more than a year. He's very reliable; he'd never just disappear. I have to find him right now, or the party will be ruined. His assistant says she has things under control, but she's new and not anywhere near ready to take on a gathering of this size."

Liam put a hand on her shoulder, and she tried not to notice it. She was an independent business owner, not somebody who needed reassuring.

Except…right at this moment, with a thousand guests already here, who would find *no food to eat*, yeah. She'd take whatever reassurance she could get.

"Alaric and I will take the palace. We'll find out—discreetly—if any other jewels are missing. I can get into

Riley's room with nobody suspecting anything, since she's my sister," Quinn said. "Alaric, you come with me."

"And do what? The queen won't want me in her room when she's dressing," Alaric pointed out.

"Just glower at somebody, then. You're awesome at that," Quinn said, grinning up at him.

Jaime watched the byplay between them with something that felt a lot like envy, her throat suddenly tight.

When do I get to be the one with somebody crazy about me?

Ven cleared his throat to get everyone's attention. "Okay. I'll go tell Conlan what's going on. Don't want to have to listen to him whining about how 'the king should be in on things' later."

"Let. Me. Down," Denal gritted out, from up near the ceiling, where Jaime had almost forgotten about him. Alaric twirled a single finger—and not a very *nice* finger—and Denal floated down in sort of a contained crash. He scowled at everyone, especially Alaric, and then pinned Liam with a dark stare. There seemed to be some unpleasant history between the two of them, but Jaime didn't have time to worry about it.

"I'll just go check in with your brother," Denal said, in a nasty tone that surprised Jaime.

Liam shrugged. "Fine. But he would not do this. He'd do many things, but not *this*. Everyone—even lowlifes and thieves—loves our new queen."

"Apparently not everyone." Denal pointed to the crown in Ven's hand.

"My brothers do," Liam said with finality. "Jaime, the two of us will go search for the caterer."

Jaime, all but dancing in impatience—now just D minus one hour till the party, if D Equaled Disaster—just nodded and rushed out the door, with Liam following her.

"Where should we look? Oh, crap, oh, crap, I so don't have time for this. How are we going to search all of Atlantis? Where could he even be? Why would he do this to me? What can I do--"

Liam caught up to her at the end of the hallway and ended her stream of words by pinning her against a wall and taking her mouth in a fierce, deep kiss. By the time he lifted his head, Jaime was no longer sure that she needed a caterer, or cared about a caterer, or, in fact, even remembered what the word caterer meant.

Really, she only wanted to drag Liam off to her guest room in the palace, lock the door, and strip him out of his clothes.

With her teeth.

She had to clench her thighs together at the thought, which made her moan, and that in turn made Liam's eyes darken. He bent his head to kiss her again, but she pushed him away with what remained of her willpower.

"No. No, no, no. Caterer. Now. We feed these people, or I'm ruined. The party is ruined. Life as we know it is ruined."

Liam laughed, but he let her go. "Perhaps a slight exaggeration, but I understand your point. Now. Is he a slacker? Would he be off taking a nap somewhere? Is it possible he'd be getting more supplies or food or something?"

"No, not a slacker, definitely. Not a nap. He loaded in all the supplies yesterday," she said, trying not to bite her fingernails or clutch her head or any of the other "oh, my goodness, the world is falling in" nervous habits she'd picked up over the course of running a party-planning business.

"Is he a drinker? Would he be off getting drunk?"

Jaime bristled. "No! Would I hire a drunk? Would I work

with a drunk on any event, not to mention the biggest event of my career? What do you take me for? Robert is perfectly reliable."

"Got it. Not a drunk. Would he--"

"Wait," Jaime interrupted, feeling a tiny tendril of hope. "Drink. The wines. Riley told me that the palace would provide the wines. Maybe he got caught up in the wine cellar, picking out bottles? Do you even have a wine cellar, since it's an island? How did that work when you were underwater? I guess the cold ocean would keep the chilled wines cold, but what about the others?"

Liam's eyes widened, and she realized she was babbling again. "Sorry. Nervous habit. Wine cellar—yes or no?"

"Yes, but no," he told her, taking her arm and starting off down one marble hallway at a fast pace. "Wine room, not cellar. It's the size of one of your football fields. It's possible he could have gotten lost in there. Let's go check it out."

She practically had to run to keep up with him, but that was fine. As long as Robert was in the wine cellar/room/stadium, everything was going to be perfectly fine.

*W*rong again.

CHAPTER 6

Liam watched Jaime skid to a stop just inside the oversized wooden doors to the wine room, her mouth falling open.

"This—this is the wine room?" She looked around the enormous space, filled with rows and rows of rack upon rack of bottles of wine. He guessed he'd understated things. It wasn't the size of a football field, so much. More the size of a football stadium.

"Yes." He inhaled deeply. "I've always loved the smell in here. Oak and earth and fruit and happiness."

She tilted her head and looked at him, and he suddenly felt like an idiot. Her biggest job was on the line, her caterer was missing, and he was making stupid comments about smells and happiness.

He shoved his hands in his pockets. "So. Let's just start looking."

Jaime put a hand on his arm. "I think...I mean, if you want to...I'd like to spend some time with you—get to know you more—when the party is over. Before I have to go home, I mean."

She was blushing furiously the entire time she was talking, and he found himself leaning toward her, wanting to touch her. Comfort her. Hold her.

Not wanting to think about the day she'd leave Atlantis and go back to Chicago.

"I'd like that, too. A lot. A whole helluva lot. So let's find this guy," he said with ramped-up enthusiasm. "What's his name, anyway?"

"Robert. Bob. Bob McGinty." Her eyes widened. "Ack. *Bob*. We need to find Bob. Stop distracting me with your gorgeousness!"

Before he could pursue *that* interesting line of conversation, she took off at a jog down the middle aisle. "Bob! Bob, are you in here? Bob!"

"I'll take this other aisle," Liam told her, still a little smug from that 'gorgeousness' comment.

They split up and started marching up and down the aisles of the wine room, calling out for the missing caterer. This hadn't seemed to be all that urgent before, because the man was probably just busy elsewhere or taking a break, but the stolen crown, combined with the missing man, was just too big of a coincidence to dismiss.

And Liam hated coincidence.

From a few aisles to his right, Jaime suddenly shrieked. "Oh, no. Bob! Liam, help!"

Liam took off running. When he rounded the corner of the Cabernet aisle he almost ran into the man squirming and grunting in a tied-up heap on the floor.

Jaime kneeled down and started tentatively pulling at the tape across the man's mouth, but by the way Bob's eyes were bulging he didn't appreciate her efforts. Liam gently nudged her aside, reached down, and ripped the tape off in one quick motion.

"Ouch!" Bob yelled, glaring at Liam. "You couldn't have gotten some olive oil and worked it off slowly?"

"Man up," Liam advised. "You might want to thank Jaime for coming to find your unappreciative ass, while you're at it."

Bob stopped squirming and cast a guilty glance at Jaime. "I do appreciate it. Thanks, Jaime. But get me out of these ropes, please. I have food to prepare--"

"We're past preparing, Bob. Your assistant has been on that. The party people are already here," Jaime said, tugging at the ropes around her caterer's wrists. "Liam, help?"

Liam drew his dagger and started slicing the ropes, taking care to avoid cutting the man wearing them. But speaking of ropes...

"Why exactly are you tied up in the wine room, Bob?" He gave the man a relatively mild look, but Bob—who was fairly short and looked like he enjoyed eating the fruits of his labor a little more than he should—suddenly found the floor so fascinating that he had to stare at it.

"I didn't mean to cause trouble," he said, a dark red flush creeping up his face. "I might have, ah, I might have, well--"

"Just spit it out, Bob, we're on a deadline here," Liam told him. "There. That's the last rope. A damn good job of tying knots, I've gotta admit. Whoever tied you up was either a sailor or an Atlantean."

"Or a Girl Scout," Jaime said. "I was a Girl Scout."

"A what?" He couldn't think of any explanation that made sense for the term. She scouted for missing girls, maybe?

"We dressed up in cute uniforms and did community service projects. We sold cookies, too," she said. "I was top salesperson in my troop three years in a row. The trouble, Bob?"

"I just, well, I was boasting a little bit, maybe, to the palace chef about my food."

Jaime stood up, frowning, and put her hands on her hips. "Oh, Bob, you didn't. You know better. What's the rule?"

Liam grasped Bob's hand and pulled the man up off the floor. "There's a rule?"

"We don't insult the establishment's regular cooks or chefs," Bob mumbled, looking at his shoes.

The top of the man's head came up to Liam's shoulder, and Liam knew the palace chef. She was a large, strapping woman who topped six feet, who'd scared the pants off him and his brothers when they were was small. She'd wipe the floor with this one.

Or, more to the point, tie him up and dump him in the wine room.

Liam had to clench his jaw shut to keep from bursting into laughter. "I'm guessing that Brigheda took exception to your comments?"

"She said she'd be damned to the nine hells if a popinjay of a human upstart was going to cook for HER guests," Bob muttered. "And then she punched me in the stomach, and everything went kind of dark. When I woke up, I was here, with the ropes and the tape, and she was gone."

"Now we need to be gone," Jaime snapped, tapping her foot. "We're out of time, out of time, out of time."

She started down the aisle toward the door, leaving Liam and Bob to follow after her.

"But it's *my* job. And she's doing the entire dinner for the special guests, so I don't get why she was so mad. I'm only doing the appetizers for the ordinary party guests," Bob whined. "I don't think I can finish, Jaime. I really need to head home and rest from this ordeal. In fact, I might need to go to the hospital. You have insurance, don't you?"

Liam's budding dislike for the man increased by a factor of ten thousand when he caught sight of Jaime's panicked face.

"Bob, you can't do this to me. We've got to get through this day. You're fine. You're really completely fine, just a little blow to your pride, and--"

But now that the puffed-up little man saw Jaime's desperation, he dug in his heels even more. "No. I'm sure I need medical attention. Right now. And not your woo woo healers," he said, shooting a suspicious glare at Liam. "A real doctor."

Liam took a moment to enjoy the thought of what Alaric would do to someone who called him a woo woo healer, and then he grabbed Bob by the neck.

Jaime yelped. "What are you doing? I'll never get him to work now!"

"Shh," Liam said. "I'll just be a moment, and then it will all be fine, won't it, Bob?"

Bob, whose face was turning purple even though Liam's grasp on his neck was fairly gentle, shook his head wildly and made bizarre grunting noises.

"Look in my eyes, Bob," Liam said calmly.

Bob did.

Then Bob stopped struggling.

Bob was toast.

"You came down here to find a special bottle of wine," Liam said, the *push* silken in his voice and in Bob's mind.

"I came down here to find a special bottle of wine," Bob agreed, his eyes gone vague and unfocused.

Liam nodded, let go of the man's neck, and put a little

extra oomph into his mental push. "You bumped your head on the edge of a rack, but it's nothing."

"Nothing."

Liam could tell Jaime was about to yell at him, so he shot a look at her. She scowled at him, but she stayed quiet.

"Bob, you're going to put on the best spread you've ever done in your life."

Bob nodded. "Best ever."

"And if Brigheda shows up again, you'll compliment her profusely," Liam concluded, still holding Bob's mind.

"Lovely Brigheda," Bob said, with a huge goofy smile.

"Now *go*," Liam commanded, and the caterer immediately snapped out of the trance.

"Jaime? What are you doing down here? We have to get to work right now." Bob looked wildly around, as if unsure what was happening. "I was just getting a special bottle of wine..."

Jaime's head whipped around, and she glared at Liam. "We're going to talk, and don't you forget it."

Liam nodded. He'd expected she'd be angry, but he didn't mind so much if his interference could help take some of the stress off her shoulders.

Bob called out a rushed goodbye and hurried off in a determined stride, his bald head shining.

"He should be fine now," Liam said. "Good as new. Better, even. At least for today."

"I hope so." Jaime said, sighing. "And Liam?"

He squared his shoulders. Time to take it like a man. People hated it when he messed with memories.

But those big dark eyes of hers were sparkling. "Thank you."

"You're welcome," he managed. She'd *thanked* him? She

wasn't yelling at him about how his gift was dangerous or even evil? About how *he* was evil?

She raised up on her toes and kissed his cheek. "You're amazing. And scary. You did that for me, though, and I know it, and, so, I know it's selfish, but I'm going with amazing."

She turned around, but he caught her arm and pulled her into his arms. "Oh, no. You don't get to call a man amazing and then run."

"But--"

Liam knew she was busy, and frantic, and stressed. He knew she was late, late, late. So he took her lips in a quick, hard kiss—a claiming kiss—and then he let her go. She touched her lips with her finger, smiled at him, and then she was off, practically running.

He grinned like an idiot all the way back down the hall.

CHAPTER 7

J aime ran all the way to the giant tent they'd set up and compartmented to serve as dressing rooms for those guests who hadn't brought their own costumes. There were already people milling around outside, looking confused and a little annoyed, and the entrance to the tent was still tied closed.

That didn't make sense, because she'd hired two temporary staff people to open the tent and work the costumes. She managed not to scream with frustration, even though she was throwing a big-ass tantrum on the inside. On the *outside*, though, she strode calmly over to the tent, projecting the air of confidence that she'd found was half the battle with party planning.

"I'll just be a moment, everyone," she called out, smiling at the crowd.

Then she ducked inside the tent, and all calm and all confidence immediately vanished from existence—just like her prospects for a future career after this nightmare of a day—because *nobody was there.*

"Where are you? Sanchez? Williams? I need you up front *right now*."

Nobody answered, but she saw that one of the fitting room doors was hanging half-shut and askew. She automatically headed across the room to straighten it out, but then she saw her third horrifying sight of the day: Sanchez and Williams, lying crumpled on the ground half in and half out of the fitting room.

She snapped out of her shock, ran over, and knelt down to check her people. They were both still breathing, thankfully, and she gave a deep sigh of relief at that. Sanchez had a horrible bruise on one side of his face, though, and there was a little blood in Williams's hair. Neither of them roused when she tried gently shaking them, so she stopped in case the shaking caused further injury.

She fumbled for the communications device on her belt. The queen had given it to Jaime when she first came to stay.

"I need help right now, please. Someone has attacked my staff. We're in the costumes tent. Please hurry!"

To her surprise, Liam answered. "Get out *right now*. The attackers might still be there."

She jumped up and whirled around, belatedly realizing that she may have been in danger, but there really wasn't anywhere for anyone to hide. The fitting room doors were all tied open. The rack of costumes along the wall nearest them had been ransacked, though. Costumes had been ripped off hangers and hurled on the floor, which was *not* the way she'd left them.

"No, it's empty except for us. We need help, though. Sanchez and Williams are injured. Please hurry."

"I'm on the way," Liam said, and it sounded like he was running while talking.

"Bring a medical team or healer, please. Woo woo or otherwise. And, Liam?"

He burst in to the tent, still holding the communicator. "What? Are you hurt?"

She took her first full breath since she'd seen Sanchez and Williams on the floor and ran toward him. She wasn't sure when or how the knowledge had settled into her bones, but she'd known Liam would help. Help her get care for her guys—help with everything.

She might not be a damsel in distress, but everybody needed someone she could count on. It didn't make any sense at all, but for the first time in forever, she finally felt like she'd found her someone.

Before she could speak, Liam pulled her into his arms and held her close. "Are you hurt, *mi bella*? Please tell me you're okay."

She felt the tremor in his big body, and she realized that he'd been afraid for her. Warmth swept through her, and her throat started to hurt. She took a deep, shuddering breath, and realized that she was about half a second from crying all over him.

So she pushed him away, to stand on her own two feet. That's what Radcliffes did, after all. They were strong. Independent.

Lonely, her traitorous heart whispered. But she didn't have time for hearts. She had a party to run and criminals to find.

"I'm fine. It's Sanchez and Williams. Somebody knocked them out, and it looks like whoever did it rummaged through the costumes, which is weird. We made it clear on the invitation that there is no charge to wear a costume."

The corners of Liam's mouth kicked up, but he still looked grim. "I doubt this is about Halloween costumes,

Jaime. What are costumes but disguises? And now we know we have more than one culprit in the jewel theft."

Her eyes widened, but she immediately understood. "You think the thieves came for costumes to wear to make their escapes. They did this to my people so they wouldn't recognize them and so can't identify them, or would at least be out cold until the bad guys escape."

Liam checked the pulses of the two on the floor, and then he nodded. "Yes. And we have no way to know which costumes they stole, so they could be anywhere in that horde of people out there, with whatever else they've stolen from the palace."

"This is so frustrating," Jaime groaned. "I want to smash something."

"I feel the same way. Maybe we should have saved some of your fruit," Liam said ruefully. "This day, which started out in such a promising way, has turned into a *mierde* fest of the highest caliber."

A muscle clenched in his jaw, and Jaime wanted to reassure him, but then another—much worse—thought struck. He'd been so sure his brother wasn't involved, before. But what if Denal had been right? She'd never met his family...

"Liam? I don't want to even bring this up, but when Denal was talking about your family, there seemed to be some pretty fierce hostility there. You don't think—I mean, of course you don't—but, well, is there anything--"

He laughed, but it was a harsh and bitter sound. "No. I don't want to talk about my family, but since you brought it up...Stealing crown jewels? Definitely not Dare's style. But this? Knocking a couple of humans on the head to abscond with Halloween costumes for some undoubtedly wild-ass prank?" Liam grimaced. "This actually has Dare's name written all over it."

"Dare?"

"My idiot brother," he said, biting off the words. Then he thought about what exactly he'd do if his family came between him and his mission, yet again...

He didn't realize he was swearing out loud until Jaime put a hand on his arm.

"Hey. I don't know what language you're speaking—it's not my classroom French, that's for sure—but I just wanted to apologize for bringing up a sore subject. I'm sure your family isn't involved, if they're anything like you at all."

Liam stared down at her, and she was almost sure she saw something like shock in his eyes. "Thank you," he finally said.

"You're welcome, but where is the medical team?"

A cold wind whipped Jaime's hair away from her face, and Alaric appeared.

"The medical team is here," he proclaimed.

Something about Alaric made *everything* he said sound like a proclamation; an observation she was sure he wouldn't appreciate.

Before she could stick her foot in her mouth by saying it anyway, the ex-high priest waved his hands over the men. A dome-like flare of intense blue light spread over the two. Within seconds, they were both awake and sitting up.

"What's going on, Jaime?" Sanchez rubbed the back of his head. "I was having a strange dream...Wait. Those three people. A woman and two men. They came in and--"

"They knocked us out," Williams interrupted, outrage plain in his voice.

The two of them climbed to their feet, and Jaime was relieved to see how steady they were—as if nothing had happened to them at all.

"Thank you so much. You're a miracle worker," she told Alaric.

He merely raised an eyebrow before turning back to the men. "Tell us everything."

But they didn't have much to say. The three people had come in wearing masks of dead American presidents, which Sanchez and Williams hadn't thought much about, since this was a costume party.

"Two Washingtons and a Lincoln, I'm guessing," Jaime said, spotting the discarded masks on the floor on top of a pile of discarded costumes.

Sanchez scowled. "Yeah. Then the big guy pulls a stick, like a police baton, out of somewhere and knocks Williams out. I tried to help, but the woman got behind me somehow, and next thing I knew, *pow.*"

"Pow, indeed," said Alaric, looking scarier than ever.

Both Williams and Sanchez backed away from Alaric—slowly—and turned to Jaime. "Anyway, we're fine, boss. We'll get back to work now and get these guests in costumes in no time."

Sanchez held out his hand to Alaric, looking only slightly nervous. "Thanks, man."

Alaric was silent for a long moment. Just when Jaime was starting to get nervous, he shook Sanchez's hand. "You are very welcome."

Williams added his thanks, and the two men headed to the front area to set up.

"In all these people, we'll never find them. We don't even know what costumes they took."

Jaime started to smile. "That's not exactly true."

"What did you mean by 'that's not exactly true'? Do you have a way to figure out which costumes are missing?" Liam's hand went to the hilt of his dagger, and she had no doubt that if the thieves showed up now, they were going to regret it for a very long time.

Costumes. *Right*. She nodded. "Of course. I have them all inventoried by type and size, since I rented them from the best costume shop in Chicago. We just need to hang up these on the floor, and I'll easily be able to see what's gone."

Liam grabbed her shoulders and kissed her, right there in front of Alaric and her staff. A toe-tingling kind of kiss.

"Liam, you can't just--"

"Yes I can," he said, a purely male look of satisfaction on his gorgeous face.

"Perhaps we could save the displays of personal affection for a later time," Alaric said coldly. "And discover the culprits now?"

Jaime could feel her face heating up, but Liam just grinned. The man must have nerves of steel.

"Got it. I'll be sure to remind you that you said that the next time I see you kissing Quinn in the garden," Liam said.

Alaric bared his teeth in a grimace, and Jaime decided it was time to intervene.

"Here's what we do. Although it would be better if I had some help..."

Just then, the tent flap opened and five men and women hurried into the tent. "Lady Quinn sent us, my lord," one of them told Alaric, bowing deeply. "We're here to help in any way we can."

Alaric pointed at Liam, who took charge. "Perfect. Thanks. Jaime will tell you what we need. I'm going to assign guards to this tent and to the visitor docks. I've already asked for extra guards at the palace, and especially at the doors of the family wings."

"Please thank Quinn, er, Lady Quinn, for the help, Alaric —um, your Lordliness," Jaime said, perfectly polite but distracted by the task of searching the forms on her tablet for the costume inventory. "Okay. Here it is. Let's get everything hung back up; you can tell by size and type of costume where they go."

The Atlanteans set to work swiftly and efficiently, and within minutes, they had their answer.

"A princess, a pirate, and a ninja are missing," Jaime announced. "We just have to look for those. And I can show you exactly what those costumes look like, because we have the identical ones here in many different sizes."

Liam blew out a breath. "Sure. No problem. Except on my way here, I saw hundreds of people in costume, and I'm sure there were multiple princesses and at least two pirates. Even with the details of what colors they are, it's going to be hard to find them I didn't see any ninjas, though, which is probably good. Ninja costumes are fairly generic, right? That one will be tougher to single out."

"I saw a ninja," Alaric said, frowning. "However, I find the custom of appropriating another culture's manner of clothing for entertainment to be distasteful. Also, the ninja asked me for candy."

"Did you blast him?" Jaime asked, momentarily diverted.

"No. I did not *blast* him. He was a *child*," Alaric said.

"Probably not our culprit, then," Liam pointed out, and Jaime had to clamp her mouth shut to avoid laughing. Alaric probably would have no problem blasting *her*. "The big question is this: How do we isolate *our* princess, pirate, and ninja from the herd?"

Jaime only had to think about it for ten seconds before it hit her: "We have a costume contest! But only princesses, pirates, and ninjas are eligible."

CHAPTER 8

Liam's shoulders slumped. The stress was clearly getting to Jaime. "A costume contest?"

"I know, it sounds ridiculous, but listen: we announce that the top three prizes go to a princess, a pirate, and a ninja. See?"

"No. I don't see."

She grabbed his arm. "The thieves aren't going to show up for the prizes, so we'll be able to more easily find them in the crowd. The costumes make perfect sense; don't you think?"

Alaric narrowed his eyes. "No. Explain. Now."

"Well, if they stole more jewels, which we don't know yet--"

"Which *you* don't know yet," Alaric told her, which ticked Liam off.

"Look," he said, before Alaric could annoy him again. "If you know something, you need to tell us."

Jaime's smile was brilliant. "There's an *us*? Let's definitely make time to talk."

Alaric's warning growl snapped the stupid smile right off Liam's face.

"Princesses and pirates wear and carry jewels," Jaime explained in a rush. "And a ninja has a face mask to help hide his identity. They're perfect."

"Well, let's go make it unperfect," Liam said.

"Agreed," Alaric said. "I'll inform the guards of the plan."

With that, the priest sliced one hand through the air, which opened up a straight line in the fabric of the back of the tent, and then he exited through it.

"I'll have to pay for that plus the missing costumes," Jaime muttered, looking hopeless.

Seconds later, though, the tent fabric wove itself back together, good as new.

You're welcome, said Alaric's disembodied voice on the Atlantean shared mental pathway.

Jaime jumped. "Did he just put his voice in my *head*? That's so creepy."

Liam's interest sharpened. "You heard that?"

"Yes. Didn't you?"

"Only Atlanteans, or those who share the Atlantean gene, can communicate via the mental pathway," he told her.

Do you hear me, too, or was it just him?

Her eyes widened. "You can do it, too? That's wild. I wonder if I can do it. Let's remember to figure it all out once we find our thieves, okay?"

"Deal."

The first party goers in need of costumes entered the tent then so, after Jaime made sure that Sanchez and Williams were following the system she'd set in place, Liam took her hand and they followed the music to the temporary stage that had been set up just outside the palace gardens.

The Atlantis orchestra was playing one of its original compositions, and the group around the stage was one part appreciative listeners and dancers, and one part crazed musical scholars. The discovery that Atlantis actually existed and had maintained a separate civilization for more than eleven thousand years had been news of mammoth proportions to academics of all kinds. Every day, more and more researchers applied for permission to come and study —historians, archaeologists, and anthropologists had been first, but linguists, musical theorists, and literature professors hadn't been far behind.

"Oh, Liam, that's so beautiful," Jaime said, sighing. "I feel like I could happily spend the next ten years doing nothing but sitting here listening to this music. If only--"

Suddenly—impossibly—Liam wanted to ask her to dance. To feel her head nestled against his shoulder; to waltz with her across the floor until their problems and even the world itself fell away beneath the sound of the music and the beating of his heart.

Every muscle in his body tensed at the realization that he was falling, and falling *hard*, for this woman. He'd only had a handful of conversations with her during the weeks she'd been in Atlantis, but her courage, resourcefulness, and ability to retain her sense of humor under intense pressure intrigued and impressed him. She was beautiful; hells yes, he admitted to himself.

But she was also something more.

The *something more* was what had him tangled up in knots. Once they caught these damned thieves, he was going to drag Jaime off somewhere private and explore every bit of the powerful attraction between them.

The orchestra finished its set, and Liam leapt up on the stage to have a word with the director. Jaime followed him by way of the steps, and when she reached him, he put the microphone in her hands.

"This is your party, so maybe it should come from you," he said into her ear, so the mike didn't pick up his words.

She took a deep breath and nodded and then, right before his eyes, transformed back into perfect professional party planner mode.

"Happy Halloween, everyone!" She gestured at the garden and palace with a flourish. "We're so pleased to welcome you to Atlantis."

Everyone cheered. Liam scanned the crowd for any pirates, princesses, or ninjas, and he found them. Lots of them. He could see at least five princesses from here. Plenty of superheroes, too, which was entertaining, given that so many of Poseidon's sworn warriors—far more badass than any superhero--were in attendance, as well.

"I'd kick that bat guy's ass," he told Jaime, who gave him a puzzled look, shushed him, and turned back to the waiting crowd.

"King Conlan and Queen Riley will be here soon to welcome you officially, and until then, we'd love for you to all relax, enjoy the wonderful food and drink, and the lovely music. But first, we have a surprise!"

When everyone applauded, Jaime put a surreptitious hand over the top of the mike. "Here we go. Are your guards in place to look for any pirates, etc., who might start running in the opposite direction?"

Liam opened his mind to find Alaric on the mental pathway:

We're ready to go—everything all set.

Two seconds later, Alaric replied with a single word:

Go.

Jaime looked a question at him, and Liam nodded. They were ready.

"Okay, everyone. This is so exciting! We're having a surprise mini-costume contest in addition to the overall costume contest later this evening. Judges from Atlantis have been casting their ballots in secret and we have three winners: a pirate, a ninja, and a princess!"

There was more applause, but mostly everyone was turning to look at everyone else, and some of the people in variations of those costumes started heading for the stage. Nobody was stupid enough to scream "you'll never catch me" and start running, unfortunately.

It was always easier when the criminals were stupid.

Ven's voice came through on the pathway:

We've got one of them. Found a ninja hiding in a speedboat at the guest dock. He's spilling the beans on the other two, under Denal's gentle questioning. Hey, Liam, Dare is here, too.

Liam felt like Ven had just punched him in the gut. His brother *was* involved. His entire future just swirled down the drain. Before he could even think of how to respond, Ven came through again:

Sorry, I should have clarified. Dare helped us find this one and is going to assist in the search for the others.

Jaime glanced at him, and her eyes widened with real alarm. "Liam, are you okay? You look--"

"I'm fine," he said. "Family stuff. Tell you later."

Because, much to his surprise, he realized he actually did want to tell her about his family, and his childhood, and his life. He wanted to talk to her for hours and listen to her for days and hold her in his arms for...

This time, it was his *own* voice he heard in his mind:

Where in the nine hells did that come from? Hold her forever? *Time to get your head back in the game, dumbass.*

"They've got one of them," he told Jaime. "I need to go help find the others. You stay here and do this, and I'll find someone to help."

He scanned the crowd again, this time looking for familiar faces, and was relieved to spot Erin, Ven's wife, standing at the edge of the dance floor and looking amused.

He leaned over to speak into Jaime's microphone. "Erin Connors, will you please report to the stage?"

Erin raised an eyebrow, but gamely cooperated with his request. When she'd climbed the stairs to the steps, he bowed.

"Lady Erin, my apologies, but we need your help. Will you please assist Jaime with the costume contest while I go help Ven and the others track down our missing...friends?"

Erin was a whole lot of personality and attitude packaged in a small package—and she was a witch. The magical kind. He didn't know her well, but everyone he knew was half in love with her. Only half, because Ven wasn't called the King's Vengeance for nothing.

She nodded. "Sure. Hi, Jaime. Nice to see you again. Liam, if you call me Lady Erin again, I'll kick your ass for you."

He laughed. "You and your husband are well-mated."

"Hi, Erin," Jaime said, glancing back over her shoulder to scowl at Liam. "Nice to see you as well. But I'm not staying. We need you to pick three winners and promise them an extra special prize, which I'll provide if they present themselves at the costumes tent in an hour."

With that, she handed the mike over to a bemused Erin, and ran lightly off the stage and down the steps, leaving

Liam with nothing to do but thank Erin and then follow Jaime.

He caught up with her in less than half a minute. "What do you think you're doing? These people are criminals. They may be armed. You need to go somewhere safe. Like the palace. Like your rooms. Or my rooms. Yeah, that's even better. And lock the door behind you."

Jaime stopped walking and swung around to face him. "You want me to run and hide? Those were my staff guys that they attacked. I'm not an idiot. I know I'm not a warrior. I'm a party planner. But I'm darn good at my job, and I can pick out the three exact costumes we need to find faster than anybody else, since I picked them out, picked them up, and hung them up."

Liam blew out a sigh. "Two costumes."

She put her hands on her hips and raised her chin, all stormy eyes and determination. "What makes you think...wait. *What*?"

"I said two costumes. Ven and Denal caught the ninja. Now all we need are the princess and the pirate."

"The princess and the pirate." Jaime started laughing. "I bet you never expected that strange phrase to come out of your mouth."

"This is Atlantis. Trust me, I've said stranger."

CHAPTER 9

Dusk was falling rapidly, and Jaime inhaled a long, deep breath of the cool evening air with a sigh of pleasure. This was her favorite time of day in Atlantis. After all, the lost continent was now basically a giant island, right in the middle of the Bermuda Triangle. So they were surrounded by nothing but ocean and the sky, which was drenched with the rich oranges, scarlets, and golds of another perfect sunset.

And if she stared right into the sun, maybe her brain would melt, and she'd be able to forget that there were still two dangerous criminals at large.

"I can't believe I even said the expression 'criminals at large' in my mind," she muttered, as Liam led her to an almost-hidden door in the garden wall.

"Are you sure you're up for this? Why don't you just go up to the palace and--"

"Why don't you give it up, so we can catch these crooks and get on with the evening?"

He threw his hands up in the air, and she couldn't help but notice that he'd rolled up his sleeves and was treating her to a great view of the tanned, corded muscle in his bare forearms.

Also: her hormones were affecting her brain.

No muscles. Think about criminals.

"Why are we here?" she asked desperately. "Do you think they're going to be hiding in the bushes?"

"No, but there's a great view from the top of that wall, and nobody ever looks up. So I'm going to give you a boost, and you're going to search for pirates and princesses."

With that, he grasped her hips and lifted her in one smooth motion until she could grab the top of the wall.

"This is a surprisingly erotic position," Liam said, his voice filled with laughter.

She glanced down to see what he was talking about, only to realize that his face was exactly level with her butt. She was suddenly fiercely glad that it was dusk, so he couldn't see the full extent of her blush.

"Stop that and lift me higher," she demanded.

He chuckled, but then he did what she asked, until the top of the wall was level with her chest and she could easily pull herself up.

She scrambled around to a sitting position. The wall was more two feet thick, so she wasn't worried about falling off, but she did have just the teensiest problem with heights, so she refused to look down at Liam. It didn't bother her—not as much, to be exact—to look out over the grounds at people in the distance, though, so she did, and then she gasped.

"What is it? Do you see them?"

"No, it's just...it's just so beautiful from up here. All the fairy lights, and the gardens. The people and the dancing. The fountain and...oh. *Oh.*"

"What?" Liam's voice was sharp with frustrated impatience.

"There are people having sex in the garden," she admitted, feeling her stupid face heat up again. "Never mind."

Silence.

"Liam?"

He laughed. "Sorry. I was just wishing that you and I were the ones in that garden."

"Stop! I'm trying to focus here. I don't see...Liam! There they are. That must be them, get me down." Brazen as could be, a princess and a pirate were walking hand in hand to a small speedboat that was pulled up to the nearest guest dock and tied off between two much larger boats.

"Where are they?"

She looked for the twosome again. They were almost to the dock, but she and Liam were almost exactly as far away from that boat as the pirate and princess were. They could catch the criminals before they had a chance to escape.

"Liam, I'm coming down. They're almost at the dock, and they're each carrying bulging bags. I bet they stole lots of things."

"Wait--"

"I'm coming now. Catch me." They didn't have *time* to wait. She pushed off with her hands and jumped off the wall, somehow insanely sure that he'd catch her.

And of course he did.

"Don't ever do that again. You could have broken your neck," he gritted out, gently setting her down on her feet.

"They're almost to the guest dock," she told him, starting to run. "And they have big bags filled with something, and there's a small speedboat that's not supposed to be there. Plus, I knew you'd catch me."

He took off running, and there was no way she would

ever keep up with him. The man ran like a world-class sprinter, and that was in boots, for Pete's sake.

"I regret that last donut at breakfast," she called after him, panting, and then put on a burst of speed.

By the time she made it to the dock, Liam had knocked out and tied up the pirate. Convenient how there were always plenty of ropes on docks.

The princess was yelling a stream of profanity at Liam, so Jaime walked up to her and punched her in the nose.

Hard.

The princess, shocked, quit swearing at Liam and fell back against the wooden post, then slid to the ground, holding on to her nose.

"You broke by dose," she shouted.

Jaime shook her hand to try to get the stinging to stop, and it took her a few seconds to translate that one.

"I did not break your nose," she said indignantly. "I've never broken a nose in my life. But if I did, you'd deserve it."

Liam stood there staring at her with what looked like reluctant admiration. "Way to go, Slugger. We'll have to recruit you to train the warrior trainees in boxing."

"Very funny," she said sternly, but she was secretly pleased. "Now open the bags and see what they've got, please."

Alaric, Ven, Erin, and Denal all ran out onto the dock together, just in time to see Liam unzip the second bag and stand back, whistling long and loud. The dock lights reflected off what looked to Jaime like all the gold coins and gems in the world.

"How in the nine hells did they get into the gallery with the crown jewels?"

Ven shook his head. "If Fiona were here, I'd be sure she was involved."

Jaime, still shaking the soreness out of her hand, had to ask. "Fiona?"

"Christophe's wife is an international jewel thief," Liam said absently. "I'll tell you later."

"All righty," Ven said, sauntering up to the now-stirring pirate. "Time to go to jail. Consider yourself lucky that we don't make you walk the plank."

The princess started in on a fresh torrent of filthy swearing, and Liam's eyes narrowed. "Princesses don't talk that way on Atlantis."

He moved to take her arm, but Alaric intervened. "I'll take this one, warrior."

The former priest waved his hand, and the pirate and the princess vanished.

Jaime's mouth fell open. "Did you disintegrate them? Because that's just not right."

Quinn started laughing, and Alaric even almost smiled. "No, I did not disintegrate them. I am not in the habit of disintegrating humans--not even thieves."

She didn't feel all that much better about it. "But you *could* disintegrate someone?"

Alaric said nothing.

"Oh, boy," Jaime whispered. "I'm on your good side, right?"

Alaric still said nothing, but this time Quinn elbowed him in the side. "Quit playing with Liam's girlfriend."

"I'm not actually his girlfriend," Jaime pointed out.

Alaric put an arm around Quinn and pulled her close. "Where have we heard that before, my love?"

Quinn started laughing, but Jaime didn't get the joke.

"Nice job, Jaime," Denal said, smiling at her. "I'd be glad to help you with the rest of the party."

Liam spoke up, quiet but deadly. "Over my dead body."

"That can be arranged," Denal shot back at him.

Jaime stepped between the two of them and put a hand on Liam's arm. "Thanks, Denal, but we've got it covered. But I'd love it if you'd help judge the children's costume contest."

Denal raised one sardonic eyebrow and then bowed to her. "I'm not the best person to be around innocents these days. Another time, perhaps."

With that, he and everyone else left, leaving her alone with Liam.

"We did it," she told him, smiling like a loon. "We were Nancy Drew and Sherlock Holmes all wrapped up in one."

Liam tilted his head. "Who?"

"Never mind. It doesn't matter at all. You should kiss me now," she told him.

"I thought you'd never ask." With that, he leapt across the space between them and pulled her into his arms.

His kiss in the morning had been all heat and fire; this kiss was gentleness and seduction. He teased and nibbled at her lips, caught her tongue with his own, and kissed her and kissed her. She was lost, drowning, dreaming in the ever-deepening erotic temptation of this kiss, this quietly demanding kiss that didn't take but gave and gave and gave until she knew she wanted to surrender.

Needed to surrender.

Needed to claim his surrender, in return.

Liam kissed her until she could taste colors and smell music; until her world spun on its axis and only he and she —only Liam and Jaime—still existed in the vastness of time.

When he finally released his claim on her mouth, she let out a long, shivering breath and clung to him, not sure that her knees would hold her up.

"Liam, I...I have to get back to the party," she said, although it was the hardest thing she'd ever had to say.

"So let's go. I guess I need a costume," he said, taking her hand.

They started off for the tent, but this time it was Jaime's turn to laugh. "So long as you don't want to be a pirate, a ninja, or a princess."

CHAPTER 10

It was nearing midnight and the end of the party before Jaime had a chance to talk to Queen Riley and find out if she'd enjoyed it. She'd been insanely busy making sure every single bit of the party had run smoothly, especially after the fiasco of the first half. She also had to keep reminding herself that nobody but the few involved even knew that anything bad had happened.

When she was finishing the last face paint, on a tiny Wonder Woman with curly red hair and sparkly shoes, Riley and Conlan came to find her. They'd dressed as Han Solo and Princess Leia, and little Prince Aidan was a baby Wookie.

"All done," Jaime pronounced, and the littlest Amazon ran off to her patiently waiting parents.

"He's adorable," she told Aidan's royal parents. "Best costume of the night."

"We think so," Riley said, smiling. "But we're biased."

"We wanted to thank you for everything," Riley said. "This has been the most magnificent party I've ever been to, let alone ever hosted. I've firmly blocked my empath senses so I don't have any idea what anybody is feeling, which is amazing And you—*you* are absolutely incredible. Anything you want—references, a Yelp review, anything—you just name it."

King Conlan, all controlled power and presence, turned his head to look at his wife. "Yelp?"

"I'll tell you later," she said, smiling up at him.

Riley could tell that they were blissfully happy together, and she was happy for them, but they made her want to go find Liam and share a bottle of champagne.

"I appreciate it," she told the queen, instead. "That will be amazing. When I go back to Chicago."

But even saying 'back to Chicago' depressed her. She didn't want to go back to Chicago, for so many reasons. It was cold and windy and *not Atlantis.*

And maybe the biggest reason of all had ocean blue eyes and kissed like an angel.

"The best part is that there was absolutely no drama. Everything went perfectly," Riley said, sighing with contentment. "You have no idea how rare that is for me over the past several years—or how wonderful. Smooth as silk; not a hitch. I'm so happy."

Jaime had to clamp her teeth together to keep from bursting out in hysterical laughter, so she just smiled and nodded.

Riley touched her arm. "Thanks again. I'll see you at breakfast, if you're up, but feel free to sleep in. You've certainly earned it. Good night."

"Good night," Jaime managed.

As the royal family walked off toward the palace, she heard Riley repeat "smooth as silk," and the king glanced back at her.

And he *winked.*

She waited until they'd disappeared into the garden to let the laughter escape. He *knew*. And now she knew that he knew, and he knew that she knew that he...oh, forget it.

She plopped back down on the face-painting chair and laughed until her sides ached.

"Smooth as silk." She ought to put that on her business cards.

She was still laughing when Liam found her.

CHAPTER 11

When the superhero walked in, Jaime was ready.

It was two-thirty in the morning, and everything was packed up, cleaned, put away, and spotless. She'd never had an army of assistants before, but it seemed like everyone on Atlantis wanted to help out and, as her grandmother used to say, "many hands made light work." Now everyone else was gone, and she was exhausted, starving, and deliriously happy.

"I deserved some light work, after the day that we had, Batman," she told the tall, dark, and deadly warrior standing in front of her.

"I don't understand this costume," Liam replied, looking down at himself. "It would hinder me while fighting. What if the sword gets caught in this stupid cape? Then evil would win, all due to poor clothing choice."

He looked so disgruntled that she had to laugh. And then she had to kiss him.

Not here, though.

She pointed to the large basket on the table. "Maybe you

could carry that, my not-so-caped crusader? I have food, I have champagne, and I have a blanket. I was hoping we could go have a picnic at the beach, since I never got to eat."

Liam pulled the mask off his head and smiled that slow, dangerous smile that made her melt. "I'd like that very much. Just let me get rid of this damn cape."

He pulled the costume off, right there in front of her, not even a little bit bashful. Beneath it he wore only a low-riding pair of black briefs. She had to bite her lip to keep from hyperventilating over all that lean, tanned muscle, while he pulled on his pants and shirt and put his boots back on.

When he straightened, his shirt still unbuttoned, she got a glimpse of a tattoo, high on the left side of his chest. He saw her notice it, so he moved the fabric aside so she could get a better look.

"What is it?"

"This is the symbol of Poseidon's Warriors, given to me by the sea god himself. The circle represents all the peoples of the world, intersected by the pyramid of knowledge deeded to them by the ancients. The silhouette of Poseidon's Trident bisects them both."

"It's more than a job, isn't it?"

He nodded, suddenly serious. "It's a sacred vow."

She swallowed, her mouth suddenly dry. "I don't think I've ever made any vows, sacred or otherwise."

"Do you want to?"

She froze, not even knowing how to answer that question. Instead, she evaded. "I'll just go remove my costume and get dressed."

His eyes blazed so hot they glowed. "I'd be happy to help you with that."

Jaime's brain quit working entirely while she thought about *that.*

"Jaime?"

"Um." She licked her lips, and got a little dizzy when Liam's gaze arrowed in on her mouth.

"I can do that for you, too."

"Eep. I mean, later. I mean, I have to get changed," she said, grabbing the bag with her clothes.

"Wait. What *is* that costume? Not that you're not always beautiful, but why in the world are you dressed up as a blue box?"

Jaime smoothed the skirt of her dress. "Oh, Liam, you're in for a treat. I'm going to introduce you to the wonderful world of Doctor Who."

"Who?" He looked puzzled. "You're a doctor?"

"Let me get changed, and I'll tell you on the beach. I'm going to fall over if I don't get something to eat."

⁓

*L*iam watched Jaime toy with her champagne glass as she stared out over the moon-bright white sand, and he suddenly wanted her with a fierce, primal desperation. She was going to leave him, and he wanted to claim her so she could never, ever go.

It didn't even make sense. He hadn't known her long enough to make such a claim—to make *any* claim--but his heart was telling his mind to shut up.

And his soul was reaching out to her; he could feel it. He'd heard talk of the soul-meld—the earth-shatteringly intense bond that a warrior who was very, very lucky could form with his mate. He'd just never expected to feel it himself. Not with his past. Not with his family.

Every time he touched her, though, and especially when she kissed him, he could almost feel it. A silvery brilliance, spiraling inside him like water magic, reaching out to connect. He'd caught the barest glimpse in her memories of her cold and lonely childhood, and he'd instantly retreated, knowing she'd see it as intrusion. As violation.

But even that glimpse had shown him enough to help him understand. Her need to stand for herself; to be strong.

He only admired her more for it.

They'd talked for hours about nothing and everything. Sometimes he'd just watched the curve of her lips as she spoke. It wouldn't be long now before the sun rose to take her place in the sky, and he wanted to stand up and howl at the moon to stay for just a while longer.

Just another night.

Morning would bring breakfast, and other people, and commitments. It would bring him one day closer to the day she was scheduled to leave Atlantis.

"I want you to meet my family," he blurted out.

She turned to look at him, her eyes huge. "What? But you said you never wanted any woman around your family."

"I want you to know me. They're part of who I am," he admitted reluctantly.

"I'd be honored to meet them, then." She shivered, and he pushed the basket out of the way and pulled her back to sit against him, her back to his front and her legs between his, and then he wrapped his arms loosely around her waist.

She leaned back against him and sighed, the scent of her hair teasing his senses. "I could stay here forever."

"Then do it."

"I don't...I have to go back. My business, my apartment, my life—it's all in Chicago," she said, but he caught the note of wistfulness in her voice, and it ignited a small flame of hope in him.

"You could plan parties here. I'll tell everyone I know to

have a party," he said, energized. "You'll be the busiest party planner on Atlantis."

"I'd be the *only* party planner on Atlantis, she said dryly. But then she snuggled back against him, and he tightened his arms around her, knowing that he wasn't ready to let her go.

Knowing that he had no right to ask her to stay.

Fair enough. It was his move—*literally*.

"Then I'll move to Chicago. I'll find some way to do it. Surely Poseidon will release me from my vow"

She twisted in his arms so she could look at him. "What? Move? You can't leave Atlantis for Chicago. It's so beautiful here, and we're going into the freezing-wind, icy-snow season up north. You'd hate it. *I* hate it."

"Then why go?"

"I don't have a choice. Please, let's not talk about it now. Just hold me, and let's watch the sun come up."

He pulled her into his lap bent his head to hers. "I'll hold you, but let's not watch the sun come up. I don't ever want the sun to come up, if it means this night ends and you leave me."

"Liam--"

"Kiss me, Jaime," he said roughly. "Just kiss me."

When she reached for him, Liam made a silent vow that she wouldn't leave without him. He could fulfill his duty to Poseidon by protecting the humanity of Chicago.

First, though, he kept his promise to Jaime. Neither of them even noticed the sun when it finally rose.

CHAPTER 12

The wind played with Jaime's hair, tickling her face until she opened her eyes to a new day, a new month, and the realization that she didn't want to leave Atlantis.

More than that—the determination to fight for the chance to stay.

"Screw a letter of reference. I'm going for official palace party planner."

A rich, deep laugh rumbled in her ear, and she curled even closer to Liam's very warm body and took a deep breath of fresh sea air. She'd never spent the night on a beach before, and she kind of loved it.

"That's the best thing I've ever heard," he said. "Also, this is the first time in my life I've ever woken up with a woman and both of us were fully dressed."

She sat up and mock-glared at him. "Dating tip: Don't talk to the woman you wake up with about the other women in your life, unless you want her to return the favor."

His eyes widened. "There are other women you've slept with? You may be too adventurous for me."

That made her laugh. "I probably am, but you'll just have to get used to it. Also, just kissing is so amazing between the two of us that we might spontaneously combust when we get to the naked part."

Liam's eyes immediately glazed over.

"Naked part," he said reverently, and she shook her head, still smiling.

"Later. We need at least a few official dates first. Now, come on. Let's get cleaned up, so we can talk Riley into creating a job for me."

He pounced, instead, and rolled on top of her. "How about you kiss me again, first, for an hour or two, and then we go talk to the queen?"

"Well, when you put it like that..." She put her arms around his neck, but when she tried to pull him down to her, he paused.

"Jaime, I have a confession to make," he said, and she groaned.

"*Now*?"

"Now. It's kind of strange, but I thought you'd like to know."

"What is it, Liam?"

He smiled that slow, dangerous smile that he only ever gave to her. "I want to have jack-o-lanterns at our wedding."

Jaime's heart skipped a beat or two or three. She'd walked into a fairy tale, and she'd found her happily-ever-after. Finally, *finally* she'd found *her* someone.

"Liam, I wouldn't have it any other way."

THANK YOU!

Thanks so much for reading *Halloween in Atlantis*. I hope you had as much fun reading it as I did writing it.

Newsletter! Would you like to know when my next book is available, get special bonus-only-for-subscribers behind the scenes info, and win cool stuff? You can sign up for my new release e-mail list (no spam, I would never sell my mailing list, and I promise not to bombard you) at http://www.alyssaday.com, follow me on twitter at @alyssa_day, or like my Facebook page at http://facebook.com/authoralyssaday.

Review it. My family hides the chocolate if I don't mention that reviews help other readers find new books, so if you have the time, please consider leaving one for *Halloween in Atlantis*. I appreciate it!

Try my other books! You can find excerpts of all of my books at https://alyssaday.com. Read on for an excerpt from the first in my new sexy and funny Cardinal Witches series, **Alejandro's Sorceress.**

EXCERPT: ALEJANDRO'S SORCERESS BY ALYSSA DAY

Poe's Avenue, Virginia, FBI Paranormal Operations Division HQ

Alejandro cocked his shotgun and followed his teammate into the burnt and jagged opening in the side of the building, hoping that—for once—there weren't any trolls.

He hated trolls.

"Clear," Mac, already moving through the narrow hallway, called back to him. It was Mac's turn to go first. They kept score.

Lately he'd been keeping score on a lot of things. Like time. The year, two weeks, and five days since he'd seen the sunlight outside of the academy, for instance.

Not that he was counting.

Anyway, the course at the FBI's sister division, P-Ops, had kept him plenty busy.

"Shotgun! You coming or scratching your ass back there?"

"No, my friend, I was just thinking of asking your sister to scratch it for me," Alejandro said, grinning at the nickname he'd won for obvious reasons. "She reaches all the itchy parts so well."

"I will kick your ass if you get any of your itchy parts anywhere near my sister. Or she'd kick it for you. Jenny scares even me."

The sound of Mac's Glock firing three shots in rapid succession caused Alejandro to break into a run as he slapped his night-vision goggles in place.

"On my way," he called, not bothering to try to be stealthy. "Save some for me."

He caught the shifting glimmer of light in the corner of one eye and whirled around, aiming and firing in one smooth motion. Whatever it was, he missed. Too short to be a troll, so there was one mercy. If he were the type to have nightmares, he'd still be having them about the last one's breath. Green, moss-covered teeth. What the hell was *that* about? Toothpaste was cheap.

"Shotgun! Could use a little help here!" Mac sounded just the slightest bit out of breath, which was unusual for the man who'd beat the all-time speed record for the FBI's obstacle course at Quantico in an inter-agency competition. Alejandro had won a hundred bucks on that one.

He took off running, cocking the Remington as he moved. The vampire who jumped him five feet down the hall took a blast to the head. Alejandro vaulted over the disintegrating body, not wanting the acidic slime of decomposing vamp on his new shoes.

A high-pitched scream warned him of the approach from overhead of a deadly Mngwa, but he had a silver throwing knife at hand. One lethal toss later, a couple hundred pounds of mutant killer cat lay on the floor, blood gurgling out of its throat.

He skidded to a stop at the end of the corridor, not willing to rush headlong into a blind turn, and Mac called out to him again, his deep voice rough and strained. "Alejandro, if you're coming, now would be a really good time."

Alejandro instantly switched from student-taking-his-final-exam mode to deadly-predator mode. They had a code between them, he and Mac. They were only Alejandro and Maxwell to each other in the event of a dire emergency. Whatever faced Mac around that corner was no training-ground obstacle. Somebody had set a trap, and Mac was caught in it.

Alejandro was going to kick somebody's ass for this one.

He dove for the floor, rolling to the side to protect the Remington, and did a modified army crawl around the corner. The natural expectation was to look for an enemy at man-height, not on the floor or the ceiling. It's why the vampires and other supes who could climb down a building or fly always had the advantage. Nobody would expect a P-Ops rookie to come in at ankle-height.

Alejandro was far, far more than a rookie.

His first glance assessed the situation and told him everything he needed to know. A trio of wolf shifters surrounded Mac, and one of them had gotten in either a good swipe of his claws or a bite—Alejandro hoped it was only claws—and Mac was down and bleeding, his gun a crushed hunk of metal on the floor.

"Come out, come out, little human," snarled the shifter who stood with one claw-tipped foot on Mac's head.

Another was on all fours, his massive head hanging down near Mac's struggling form. As Alejandro watched, that one's long tongue snaked out as he licked blood off the side of Mac's face.

"Yummy," the shifter said in his garbled voice, and then he laughed.

It was the laugh that put Alejandro over the edge. Cool,

clear-headed, Paranormal Operations training flew out the window. Hot, primal rage from years of battling murderous vampires in San Bartolo took over. He triangulated his shots in his head a split-second before he took them.

A couple of heartbeats later, three werewolves lay dead on the ground.

"Glad you talked me into that silver shot," he said mildly, as if his partner hadn't almost died and wasn't now in danger of becoming a shifter himself.

Mac forced out a laugh and hauled himself up off the ground. "Damn wolves. I was so focused on the possibility of big, bad, and ugly that I missed the pitter-patter of little feet."

"Brownies?"

"Leprechauns. Bastards tripped me up, and the wolves jumped me when I was down."

Alejandro shook his head and then blasted a hole in the side of the building. Welcome sunlight poured in, and he stepped over the bodies of the shifters to reach his friend. "Let's move."

Mac nodded, but shrugged off Alejandro's hand. "Thanks, but screw that. We're going to walk out of here like it was no problem, and then we'll get me to the infirmary after. I don't want any of those punks laughing at us."

"There are worse things than laughter," Alejandro said, eyeing Mac's wounds. Looked like claws. He hoped.

"Yeah. Fucking leprechauns." Mac bared in his teeth in a grim imitation of a smile. "At least one of them won't be tripping anybody else, ever again."

He jerked his head to indicate the far corner, and Alejandro could just make out a small green shoe pointing at the ceiling.

Alejandro headed for the hole in the wall. He needed to get Mac to the infirmary before anything worse showed up.

"Could have been worse. Could have been trolls."

Alejandro ducked his head to exit the building, so the huge wooden club smashed into the wall instead of his skull.

"Fee, fie, foe fucking fum, little Mayan," the attacker growled in a voice deeper than the interior of a volcano and just as hot.

Alejandro hit the floor and swept a foot at the troll's ankles, sending it crashing to the ground with a resounding thud. With anything that big, the trick was to go for the feet, ankles, or knees. Before he could cock the shotgun, Mac pointed his Glock at the troll's head and shot it through one eye.

Alejandro stood up and nodded his thanks.

"I owed you one," Mac said, but he was now noticeably leaning to the right, and the blood dripping out of his wounds wasn't showing any signs of stopping.

Alejandro sighed. "Why is it always trolls?"

BOOKS BY ALYSSA

THE TIGER'S EYE MYSTERY SERIES:

Dead Eye

Private Eye

Travelling Eye *(a short story)*

Evil Eye *(coming in 2017)*

POSEIDON'S WARRIORS SERIES:

Halloween in Atlantis

Christmas in Atlantis

January in Atlantis

February in Atlantis

March in Atlantis

April in Atlantis

May in Atlantis

June in Atlantis

July in Atlantis

August in Atlantis

September in Atlantis

October in Atlantis

November in Atlantis

December in Atlantis

THE CARDINAL WITCHES SERIES:

Alejandro's Sorceress *(a novella)*

William's Witch *(a short story)*

Damon's Enchantress *(a novella)*

Jake's Djinn (a short story in the Second Chances anthology, *to be available in 2018 as a standalone)*

THE WARRIORS OF POSEIDON SERIES:

Atlantis Rising

Wild Hearts in Atlantis *(a novella; originally in the WILD THING anthology)*

Atlantis Awakening

Shifter's Lady *(a novella; originally in the SHIFTER anthology)*

Atlantis Unleashed

Atlantis Unmasked

Atlantis Redeemed

Atlantis Betrayed

Vampire in Atlantis

Heart of Atlantis

Alejandro's Sorceress *(a related novella; begins the Cardinal Witches spinoff series)*

THE LEAGUE OF THE BLACK SWAN SERIES:

The Cursed

The Curse of the Black Swan *(a novella; coming as standalone June, 2018, originally in the* ENTHRALLED *anthology)*

The Unforgiven (book canceled)

The Treasured

SHORT STORY COLLECTIONS

Random

Second Chances

NONFICTION

Email to the Front

ABOUT THE AUTHOR

Alyssa Day is the pen name (and dark and tortured alter ego) of Alesia Holliday. As Alyssa, she writes the *New York Times* and *USA Today* best-selling **Warriors of Poseidon** paranormal romance series, **Tiger's Eye Mysteries** paranormal mystery/urban fantasy series and the **Cardinal Witches** paranormal romance series. She has won many awards, including the RT BookClub Reviewer's Choice Award for Best Paranormal Romance novel of 2012. Her books have been translated into a zillion languages, but she's still holding out for Klingon.

As Alesia, she also has won many awards, including Romance Writers of America's coveted RITA award for excellence in romance fiction. Alesia writes comedies that make readers snort things out of their noses, and is the author of the award-winning memoir about military families during war-time deployments: EMAIL TO THE FRONT.

She's a diehard Buckeye who graduated *summa cum laude* from Capital University Law School and practiced as a trial lawyer in multi-million-dollar litigation for several years before coming to her senses and letting the voices in her head loose on paper. She lives somewhere near an ocean with her Navy Guy husband, two kids, and any number of rescue dogs.

You can hang out with her on Facebook

(www.facebook.com/AuthorAlyssaDay) and Twitter (@alyssa_day), where she talks about her rescue dogs and her future pug ranch, and her blog, where she talks openly about her struggles with depression and hosts Mental Health Check In Fridays (www.alyssaday.com/blog).

If you'd like to get a sneak peek at upcoming books, read continuing free short stories, hear the scoop on swag and prizes, find out where Alyssa will be making personal appearances, and more, please text 66866 to join her newsletter.

For more information:

www.alyssaday.com

Author contact info:

Website: http://alyssaday.com/home.html

Email: authoralyssaday@gmail.com

Facebook: http://www.facebook.com/authoralyssaday

Twitter: http://twitter.com/Alyssa_Day

❅ Created with Vellum

Made in the USA
Columbia, SC
22 December 2022

74838748R00135